Praise for the Kenni Low

"Fabulous fun and fantastic fried fo
mystery with another must-read hit. (Also, ı ...
Cottonwood, KY.) Don't miss this one!"

– Darynda Jones,
New York Times Bestselling Author of *Eighth Grave After Dark*

"Packed with clever plot twists, entertaining characters, and plenty of red herrings! *Fixin' To Die* is a rollicking, delightful, down-home mystery."

– Ann Charles,
USA Today Bestselling Author of the Deadwood Mystery Series

"Southern and side-splitting funny! *Fixin' To Die* has captivating characters, nosy neighbors, and is served up with a ghost and a side of murder."

– Duffy Brown,
Author of the Consignment Shop Mysteries

"This story offers up a small touch of paranormal activity that makes for a fun read...A definite '5-star,' this is a great mystery that doesn't give up the culprit until the last few pages."

– *Suspense Magazine*

"A Southern-fried mystery with a twist that'll leave you positively breathless."

– Susan M. Boyer,
USA Today Bestselling Author of *Lowcountry Book Club*

"A wonderful series filled with adventure, a ghost, and of course some romance. This is a hard book to put down."
— *Cozy Mystery Book Reviews*

"Kappes captures the charm and quirky characters of small-town Kentucky in her new mystery...a charming, funny story with exaggerated characters. The dialect-filled quirky sayings and comments bring those characters to life."
— *Lesa's Book Critiques*

"With a fantastic cast of characters and a story filled with humor and murder you won't be able to put it down."
— *Shelley's Book Case*

"Funny and lively...Before you blink you're three chapters down and you're trying to peek ahead to see what happens next. Fast moving with great characters that you wish were real so that you might be able to visit with them more often."
— *The Reading Room*

"Kappes is an incredible author who weaves fabulous stories...I can't wait to see what she comes up next in this series."
— *Community Bookstop*

"I am totally hooked. The people of Cottonwood feel like dear friends, and I enjoy reading about the latest happenings...The story is well-told, with plenty of action and suspense, along with just enough humor to take the edge off."
— *Book Babble*

TANGLED UP IN
TINSEL

**The Kenni Lowry Mystery Series
by Tonya Kappes**

FIXIN' TO DIE (#1)
SOUTHERN FRIED (#2)
AX TO GRIND (#3)
SIX FEET UNDER (#4)
DEAD AS A DOORNAIL (#5)
TANGLED UP IN TINSEL (#6)

A KENNI LOWRY MYSTERY

TANGLED UP IN TINSEL

TONYA KAPPES

HENERY PRESS

Copyright

TANGLED UP IN TINSEL
A Kenni Lowry Mystery
Part of the Henery Press Mystery Collection

First Edition | September 2018

Henery Press, LLC
www.henerypress.com

Trade Paperback ISBN-13: 978-1-63511-396-9
Digital epub ISBN-13: 978-1-63511-397-6
Kindle ISBN-13: 978-1-63511-398-3
Hardcover ISBN-13: 978-1-63511-399-0

Printed in the United States of America

*To all the friends that I consider my family
even though we aren't blood!
Thank you for your continued support,
unconditional love, and friendship.*

Chapter One

"Let's get this Christmas season kicked off!" The sound of a scratching record rose about the sounds of whistle calls and festive cheers from inside of the Hunt Club's annual Christmas Cantata. "I'm DJ Nelly. I'm excited to be the DJ at the annual Hunt Club Christmas Cantata. I'm ready to ring in the holiday season with y'all with this little ditty to start us off," DJ Nelly said into the microphone, the black headset perched on top of her head.

You better watch out, you better not cry. The music was barely heard over the residents of Cottonwood singing along as they formed a circle in the middle of the makeshift dance floor at The Moose Lodge.

DJ Nelly from WCKK, the only radio station in Cottonwood, had more than just the regular DJ happy-go-lucky voice, she had the spirit of Christmas coursing through her veins. It was strange seeing her in person and at this hour of the night, not that it was extremely late. It was eight p.m. and on a usual night all of our small town of Cottonwood would be tucked in. Especially on this cold winter night. The fact that DJ Nelly was a morning DJ, who played toe-tapping music to get me through my morning rounds, was messing with my head.

"Here you go." Finn Vincent walked up with a couple of bourbon and cokes to start off the festive occasion. The perfect set of white teeth underneath his mesmerizing smile sent my heart into a tailspin. "I'm looking forward to my first Cottonwood Christmas Cantata," he said as his eyes captured mine.

"Cheers." He held up his plastic cup to mine.

"Merry soon-to-be Christmas." I winked as we clinked our plastic cups together before we took a drink.

The strobe lights twirled and flashed with bright colors to the beat of the Christmas tunes DJ Nelly was spinning.

"I didn't realize so many kids would be here." He nodded towards the dance floor at the jumping teenagers who were singing at the top of their lungs.

"Santa Clause is Coming to Town."

I didn't blame them. Vivid memories of me doing the same thing were at the forefront of my mind. I was excited to show Finn all the wonderful traditions Cottonwood had to offer now that he wasn't just my deputy, who should love all things Cottonwood since he too served the amazing small town, but also my boyfriend. The only difference between then and now: Cottonwood had grown. Cottonwood had grown over the past year and it was practically impossible to know everyone like I used to. As the sheriff of Cottonwood, I wanted to know everyone who lived here.

"I thought those two weren't supposed to be dating?" Finn pointed at the two heads stuck together at one of the long banquet tables, which was covered with a table cloth that looked like Santa had thrown up on with all the symbols of Christmas.

"Leighann Graves and Manuel Liberty," I mused, noticing that Leighann looked a lot more grown up than the last time I'd seen her. Then, she'd come head-to-head with my five foot five inch frame. Now she appeared to have grown taller and more mature.

Leighann's long red hair was tied up in a ponytail with what looked to be silver tinsel that was used to decorate a Christmas tree. Every time Manuel swung her around, she threw her head back and let out a great peal of laughter that echoed all over the room. Seeing her happy did make me smile.

"Leighann is now eighteen." I took another sip of my drink. "Since she turned eighteen, I don't think we've gotten any calls from her parents."

"I'm talking about her parents, not her." Finn brought the cup up to his mouth and took a sip. "Look at Sean."

He gestured to one of the tables across the room where Sean and Jilly Graves were seated, alone, and furthest away from their daughter. By the looks of disgust on their faces, neither Sean or Jilly appeared to be happy that Leighann and Manuel were still an item.

Sean had his arms folded across his chest. Jilly's face was set, her mouth was clamped, and her eyes were fixed on the young couple. Across the way, I saw Juanita Liberty with her other two sons at a table about as far away from the Graves as you could get.

"Last time I spoke with Sean, he said they were going to try and get along." I straightened up and sighed loudly before I took another drink to try to chase away the stress of the job for just one night. "He said that Leighann was legally an adult now so there's really nothing they can do."

Leighann Graves graduated last year from Cottonwood High School. She wasn't one to conform to her parent's rules and when she didn't, they'd called me, Sheriff Kendrick Lowry, to go out and find her.

I wasn't sure what they expected me to do. It wasn't like the young couple was breaking the law. Plus, Manuel worked for Sean. It wasn't technically trespassing like Sean would tell me. I did the best I could to try to talk to the young kids, but that's about all I could do.

"Look at Juanita." I pointed her out to Finn.

Finn started laughing.

"What?" I asked.

"We are always so busy assessing people and their body language that we just can't enjoy a night off." He shook his head and reached over to hold my hand.

"Job hazard." I winked. "But look at them. Both families have that disgusted look on their faces."

"Why don't they like him again?" Finn asked.

We watched as the love birds got up from their seats and moseyed up to the refreshment table.

Manuel took a couple of plastic glasses full of the best darn punch around from one of the Sweet Adelines and handed it to Leighann. You know that delicious punch, the kind that's made from Neapolitan ice cream with a ton of Spirit cola poured over top of it? The sweet and tart was the perfect combination.

It was a bonus if you got a little bit of ice cream in the cup too. Plus, the Sweet Adelines were serving it from a real glass punch bowl and not just a plastic one, making it taste even better.

"I think it was because she kept running away from home to stay with Manuel, plus her sneaking out at night didn't help." I couldn't help but smile when I noticed my mama, Vivian Lowry, hand Manuel a napkin and gesture for him to use it on the little bit of punch Leighann had spilled on her chin.

Mama was always mothering someone, and, in this instance, Southern manners went a long way in her book.

Manuel was getting a dose of Mama's class in Southern manners about right now. I also couldn't help but notice Sean Graves shake his head and lean over to say something to Jilly before they both got up and walked towards the exit.

"They aren't staying long." Finn had truly gotten to be just like one of us.

It took a few months for him to understand our unspoken rules of family and friends and gossip. This was just ideal gossip between me and him.

"By the looks of Leighann and Manuel, Sean and Jilly better get used to seeing them together. Time sure hasn't stopped the chemistry between them," I said after Manuel had pulled Leighann in for a kiss.

Out of the corner of my eye, I happened to notice my Mama walk out from behind the refreshment table, collect my daddy and head right towards me and Finn.

"Over here," I called and waved my hands in the air, acting as if I was inviting them over and not waiting on her to barge in like she always did. "Where have y'all been? Do you know how hard it is to save these seats?" I asked, even though I'd seen her through the dim lights doing her duty to her Auxiliary Women's club list of volunteering.

Another one of Mama's Southern rules in life was to volunteer anywhere you could. She was on every committee she could fit into one day.

"You know your mama." Dad rolled his eyes so hard, it made his nose curl. "First, she tried on several different outfits. Then when we got here, she took on more jobs than she'd signed up for and one of them was pouring out the punch."

"Why?" I looked at Mama. "It's the Moose Lodge. It's the Hunt Club not the Sweet Adelines putting it on. You need to enjoy yourself every once in a while."

"I wasn't sure if they'd made all their money to put on the annual dance, so I was just helping out where needed." Her Southern drawl not only drew out her words to make them longer syllables, but it drew her hand up to her chest and she lightly tapped the pearl necklace around her neck.

Earlier in the year the Hunt Club puts on their annual gun show where they rent this space from the Moose and sell guns. The proceeds go to put on this annual Christmas dance where all those proceeds go towards the schools and library of Cottonwood.

"I mighswell tell you." Mama's lips pursed as her words ran together. These are words that you never wanted to hear from Mama. They had a deeper meaning when they came from her.

"Tell me what?" I encouraged her with a deep-knotted fear that I was going to regret it.

"I'm running for Snow Queen," she proclaimed with pride. A squeal of joy broke from her lips.

"You're what?" My jaw dropped.

Finn lifted his hand to his mouth in an effort to try and cover up the smile on his face.

"The fame of being on the Culinary Channel has gone to her head and now thinks she needs to run for Snow Queen." Daddy didn't sound as enthusiastic about it as Mama did.

"Shush that up," Mama scolded him. "You turn that frown upside down because people will see that you're not happy for me. That's negative."

My eyes darted between my parents. No way, shape or form was daddy going to win this battle. Yet another defeat.

Daddy took my plastic cup and downed what I had left in my drink. "Come on, Finn." Dad nudged his head towards the cash bar. "I'll buy you a drink. I'm gonna need a double."

Mama had a big ole smile on her face and graciously nodded at everyone walking by.

"What's wrong with your hand?" I asked when I noticed she did some sort of flicking motion when someone walked by and said hello to her. "I'm sure Dr. Shively is here somewhere and can take a look at that for you." I twisted around in my seat to see if I could find Camille Shively, the only doctor in Cottonwood and who could give Mama something for her twitching hand.

"Obviously you haven't been watching any of those public broadcasting shows about the Queen and how they wave to their people." She did it again. "I'm practicing. If I win, I'll be in all the parades. These will be my people." She gestured to the room. "I'm hoping to get one of the car dealerships to sponsor me and I can sit on the back of the seat of a convertible."

"You've lost your mind." I shook my head.

"What?" She drew back. "I know it's winter, but convertible cars have heat. Besides, I've been eyeballing this fur down at Lulu's Boutique and it'd go perfect with my hair coloring." She sniffled and lifted the side of her finger under her nose. "What else do I have to look forward to this Christmas?" Her voice took a sharp turn from upbeat to tearful with a few extra sniffs to drive her point home.

"Here we go," I grumbled under my held breath and drank what little cocktail was left in my cup.

Now it was my turn for a good Southern scolding. My Mama was going to tell me which way was up and right now I was on the top of that list.

"You bet, here we go," she mocked me and shook her finger. "How do you think your father feels about you leaving us on

Christmas? You're our only child. And you decide that you're going to leave us without a Christmas after all we've done for you. After all these years?"

She was so mad, she could've started a fight in an empty house.

"I guess you wouldn't know how your father feels because you're still not married and I've got no grandchildren. Thank God for that. Hallelujah!" She threw her hands in the air. "Because it's bad enough you're leaving us alone for Christmas. If we had grandchildren and you took the pleasure of spending Christmas morning with them away from you, you mightswell stick me in a nursing home and never come see me."

"Don't worry. I'll come see you once a year." I teased "Or at least make sure the girls who work there will wipe your mouth after you eat."

I patted her hand. She jerked it away from me, apparently still not amused with my jokes.

"Mama, you've pushed me to get a boyfriend. Now that Finn and I are dating, you're mad." It was a lose-lose situation with Mama if things didn't go her way.

Mama and I had the typical Southern mother/daughter relationship. It was a love/hate relationship that no matter what, in a time of need we were there for each other one-hundred percent. The problem was, she had an image of what my relationship should look like in her head, not what was real in the world.

"Yes. But I never said that you going away for Christmas was part of it. We like Finn. He's the hunkiest male in Cottonwood." Her words describing Finn made me feel icky inside because they shouldn't be coming from my mother.

No denying she was right. He was heaven on earth and his

tall, muscular six-foot frame was that of an angel. There was only one downfall. His northern accent threw me off sometimes, but he was starting to get a bit of a twang. Around here, we called it hillbilly.

"You know that we have traditions here. Them yankies don't." Mama's face drew into a pucker.

"Mama," I scolded her. "You can't be calling people from Chicago yankies. He's a northerner."

"Northerner, yankie what's the difference?" she spat in protest.

"The difference is, Finn Vincent is my boyfriend and he loves his family just as much as I love my family. That means that we have to visit them too. We live here, and I see you practically every day," I reminded her. "Besides, you were okay with it a few weeks ago."

She stuck her pointer finger up in the air.

"Christmas is once a year." She jutted that finger towards me. "Once a year," she emphasized. "A few weeks ago was just that. Now that we are down to the nitty-gritty of Christmas Day, I thought you'd've come to your senses by now and decided to stay here."

If this would've been ten years ago when I was a teenager, I'd've tried to snap that finger off her hand.

"You two look like you're having an intense conversation," Finn said and sat down in the chair between me and Mama.

He had two drinks in his hand and he slid one to me. Daddy sat on the other side of Mama. She grabbed the wine out of his hand before his hind-end hit the chair.

"I'm gonna need the full bottle," she said in a sarcastic tone.

"It's from a box," Daddy corrected her.

"What?" Her face contorted.

"The wine." Daddy's head nodded towards her glass. "It's not from a bottle. It's from a box up there."

"Good Gawd." Mama curled her lips with icy contempt. "Lord, help me. What is this world coming to?"

I shook my head and widened my eyes to let Finn know that what Mama and I had been discussing wasn't a topic that we should be talking about. Mama had made it very clear over the past few months of her disapproval for me leaving Cottonwood during the big traditional festivities. I was going to miss being here for them since I'd not missed one since birth, but it wasn't fair to Finn. One thing I've learned since dating Finn was the fact that he too had family, a big family, and they loved Christmas just as much as we did.

"Why don't we work on your waltz since I know you're going to win and have to do it in front of the entire town the night of the tree lighting?" Finn put his hand to Mama.

She giggled in a school girl way that made me roll my eyes before she took his hand. He guided her to her feet and she tucked her hand into his elbow, letting him lead her. She did that whole Queen wave, hand twitching gesture the whole way to the dance floor.

"She's lost her mind," I leaned over to my dad and whispered.

"She's alright. She's just trying to keep her mind occupied with you going out of town." Dad dropped his head and looked at his glass of wine.

He wasn't all too thrilled about me leaving for Christmas, but he'd at least accepted it.

"You know." Dad leaned back in his chair. "I remember what it was like to leave my family for the first time at Christmas when I was dating Viv." He glanced out at the dance floor.

Mama was having too good of a time while Finn waltzed her around the plywood floor to "Have Yourself a Merry Little Christmas".

"I remember how sad my own mom was, but when I left for good and moved here, that was a whole different story." Dad had uprooted his life to move to Cottonwood and it was a story he rarely told. "The look in my mama's eye is the same look in your mama's eyes. It's just a change. Viv will get used to it, but in the meantime, if she wants to be in the Snow Queen pageant to occupy her time and it makes her happy." He smiled. "Then I support her."

I reached over and took my dad's hand.

"It's only one Christmas," I assured him and gave his hand a squeeze. "I'm actually looking forward to it." I drew my hand back and wrapped it around my plastic cup. I'd only met his sister and I was looking forward to meeting the rest of his family. "He's looking forward to me meeting them."

"Honey, your Mama is worried that you're going to go up there, love it and never come back." Dad patted me on the arm. "By the way you look at that boy, I'm a little worried too."

"There's nothing to worry about." I gulped and suddenly came to the realization that the thought of ever living outside of Cottonwood never crossed my mind.

"If Finn doesn't want to live in Cottonwood his entire life, it's an issue." Dad's words didn't comfort me any.

I dragged the cup to my mouth as I watched Finn spin Mama in one direction. On the outskirt of the spin, Mama did that hand-ticking wave thing to whoever was watching and when Finn pulled her back in, she carefully placed her hand on his shoulder like she'd already had the Snow Queen crown on her head.

"Do we know who else is in the running for queen?" I asked because I silently wanted to offer up a little pray for their safety.

"No. And God bless their hearts who do run against her." Daddy took a big swig of his cocktail and planted a big smile on his face when he saw Mama coming back. "She has practice this week at the fairgrounds. Then we'll know who her competition will be."

Once Mama gets something in her head, she doesn't stop at any expense to get it. It was all part of our Southern upbringing. I wasn't too off that mark myself. Ever heard of the apple doesn't fall too far from the tree? Well, Mama was the tree and I was the apple. Only I hid my crazy better than she did.

Mama wanted me to go to college and find me a nice man to bring home to Cottonwood where I'd be in her clubs and volunteer alongside of her, but when I told her I was going to the police academy to follow in the footsteps of her dad, my Poppa, Elmer Sims, she threw a hissy fit bigger than a toddler wanting a piece of candy they couldn't have that was dangling in front of them.

"That was fun." Mama winked at Finn. I glared at her. It was one thing for her to like my boyfriend, but to blatantly flirt with him was another. And he knew it, egging her on every time.

"My pleasure." Finn kissed the top of the hand that she'd offered him.

He was good at manipulating her like putty in his fingers. It was only him that talked some sense into her when she'd stomped around for a few days insisting I was trying to kill her by not being here for Christmas. But now, it seemed she'd gotten back on the pity wagon about it.

"Now what about you?" He turned to me with an outstretched hand. "A dance around the floor?"

Before I could even answer, there was a big ruckus going on over at the snack table near the punch bowls. Manuel and a girl that wasn't Leighann were screaming at each other at the top of their lungs. Manuel grabbed Leighann by the arm and jerked her back from the girl after Leighann started screaming at her too. Finn sprinted across the room, breaking up the three in the heated argument.

"Man, you better tell her to lay off," Manuel threatened.

"Just stop it!" Leighann screamed at Manuel and then looked at the girl. "You've always been jealous of me," she said through gritted teeth. "Get out of my life! Forever!"

"No problem. You're dead to me!" The girl turned on the balls of her feet and swung around.

"What's going on?" I asked after I moseyed on over, not in too big of a hurry because Finn seemed to have it under control.

"Nothing." Manuel jerked free of Finn and tugged down on the hem of his shirt. His muscular arms flexed without him even trying. "I told you that you need to keep better friends." His mustache quivered, and he pointed to Leighann. She was visibly upset.

Angela Durst had come to Leighann's side and pulled out a Kleenex from the pocket of her Christmas vest. Angela was Sean Graves's secretary at the towing company. She'd seen Leighann grow up.

Leighann wiped her eyes while Angela rubbed Leighann's long red hair down her back. Beka, Angela's daughter walked up and asked Manuel what was going on. He didn't answer her.

"It's nothing, sheriff." Leighann gave a fake smile. "Merry Christmas."

Manuel grabbed Leighann's hand. "Let's get out of here, babe."

"Don't babe me." She jerked away but followed him anyways. "You've run off every single friend I've ever had."

"You need better friends," he said back to her.

"Are you two okay?" I asked again before they darted out the door. They didn't bother answering me.

Finn and I looked at each other.

"Do you think they're okay?" He asked me.

"I'm sure they'll be fine." Angela shrugged. "They've had worse fights than this."

"It's getting colder out there. I think the big winter storm is going to be moving in quicker than they predicted. Get this," DJ Nelly's excitement blurted out of the speakers and interrupted our conversation with Angela. "We just might have a white Christmas."

The cheers from the crowd were catching on and soon everyone in the room was singing "I'm Dreaming of a White Christmas". Even me.

"No, no, no." Finn shook his head. "No white Christmas here."

"It's beautiful when it snows in Cottonwood." I smiled with fond memories of sledding and how they had horse drawn carriages for the tree lighting ceremony.

"Not if we can't get out of here on that big bird to go see my folks." Finn's face grew stern.

"Don't worry." I brushed off the white Christmas and any notion the airport in Lexington would close down. "What does a DJ know about weather? She barely knows what today's hits are, much less how to predict snow." I laughed and tugged him out on the dancefloor.

I didn't dare say it, but it would be my luck that we'd get this big storm and here I'd be.

Chapter Two

"Gone away is the blue bird, here to stay is the new bird. We sing a love song as we go along. Walking in a winter wonderland." I couldn't stop my finger from tapping on the steering wheel of my old Wagoneer as it rattled down Free Row—what I lovingly called Broadway Street—where I lived.

Free Row was the nickname mainly because the residents that lived on Free Row lived off the commodity cheese and other perks the government gives them.

"Walking in a winter wonderland," I sang along to the catchy tune as I began my morning route around Cottonwood to make sure everyone and everything was alright with the world. At least in our little part of the world.

The Wagoneer came to a halt at the stop sign at the intersection of Broadway and Main Street.

"Can you believe it, Duke?" I rubbed down my old hound dog and gently nudged his back end towards the seat so I could see if any cars were coming down Main Street before I turned left. "Just a few more days until we go to Chicago."

Duke wagged his tail and stuck his head out the window into the bitter cold winter jet stream that'd decided to blanket the entire state. His droopy brown eyes had a little sparkle in them as his long tan ears flapped into the wind.

"Well, until I go to Chicago," I whispered because I didn't want him to hear me since he was going to have to stay with

Joelle Fischer, my best friend.

Though he wouldn't mind since she owned a food truck and he loved riding with her. Free food, who wouldn't?

"Good morning, Cottonwood. Remember last night at the Hunt Club's annual Christmas dance where I announced the weather alert?" DJ Nelly chimed in after the song with her perky voice. "Well, batten down the hatches, get those winter gloves, hats and snow boots out because I'm coming at y'all with a wee-bit of advice since a blizzard is coming. If y'all are anywhere near the Dixon's Food Town, I suggest you stop on in and get a loaf of bread and some milk. From what I hear, they've got a new shipment overnight and it won't last long. Y'all, we ain't gonna escape this winter blizzard heading straight for us in a few days. Stock up now and don't wait."

"Seriously?" I shook my head and pulled the Jeep out on Main Street and headed north towards downtown. "Every year they say the big blizzard is coming and we get a dusting of snow. A dusting, just like powdered sugar that Ben's Diner puts on the waffles." My mouth started to water. "Man, waffles sound good about right now," I talked to Duke like he was going to answer me. "Ain't that right, Duke?"

Rowl, rowl. His feet danced on the seat to get a little more balance to avoid smacking into the dashboard when I turned the wheel.

"And while you're there, be sure to grab a shovel and some salt. Excuse me for yawning, y'all kept me out a little too late last night. You're listening to WCKK for all your Christmas tunes." DJ Nelly clicked off and so did I.

"If she thinks that a little snow is going to stop me from going to Chicago and spend Christmas with Finn and his family, she's got another thing coming and I don't want to listen." I gripped the wheel and looked up. "So, if you can hear me," I should've summoned the big guy in the sky, but I didn't. I summoned the other big guy in the sky that I personally knew and that had come to visit me a time or two in the afterlife, Elmer Sims, my Poppa. "Not that I want you to come because of a murder, but I'd like to go meet Finn's family. So why not grant me this one wish and stop any snow coming." I looked at Duke. "That should do it."

I was confident that there wasn't going to be any snow. There couldn't. Not after all the planning Finn and I had done to go to great lengths to make it happen over the past few months. Being sheriff of Cottonwood and Finley Vincent being my only deputy made it hard for both of us to take a day off, much less a few days off.

The Wagoneer headed up Main Street and I couldn't help but slow down to look at the carriage lights that dotted each side of the street. The Beautification committee had not only hung beautiful and full poinsettias on the rods next to the hung "Christmas in Cottonwood" banners, they also strung white twinkling lights up the poles. It was strange to imagine myself not waking up on Christmas morning, heading down to Ben's Diner and serving food to the homeless or taking food to the shelter.

The stop light turned yellow, slowing me down to a stop at the intersection of Chestnut Street and Main Street. To the left of me was Cowboy's Catfish, where the city rented the back portion of the restaurant for the sheriff's department. It wasn't a conventional copshop, but nothing in our small town was conventional. White's Jewelry was next to Cowboy's, next to that was Tattered Cover Books and Inn, the only place to stay downtown. Beyond that was Ben's Diner. All of their display windows were decorated with Christmas decorations and lights. The Tattered Cover had green wreaths with big red bows on each window of the three-story brick building.

A smile grew on my face when I imagined what would happen if there was a big snow storm. Downtown would look amazing and much like a winter wonderland you'd see in a fancy winter painting of a quaint small town.

Across the street there was Ruby's Antiques, that brought visitors from all over the state for Ruby Smith's delicious treasures. Kim's Buffet, a local family-owned Chinese restaurant, was next to Ruby's. Along with the radio station where DJ Nelly was all too happy giving the news of the upcoming weather I refused to even speak of.

I forced the images of the weather report to the back of my head. I'd heard Chicago was amazing this time of the year. Finn had mentioned something about going to see *The Nutcracker* and I really wanted to go.

Finn was from Chicago and had been a deputy with the Kentucky State Reserve. He'd worked a homicide with me here in Cottonwood and we just so happened to have an opening for a deputy. A few short months later, we were working side by side and we couldn't deny the chemistry between us much longer, so we started dating. In the spring, he'd asked me to go to Chicago for Christmas to meet his family. It was a no-brainer. Now that it was a few days away, no way was an over-exaggerated weather forecast nor excited DJ on the radio going to stop our trip.

It'd taken a few steps, along with a couple of headaches and campaign promises, to get City Council to approve the request for us to leave and for the State Reserve to send us an officer to fill in for us since it was Christmas. Now...getting my Mama to accept me not being here was an act of congress that still hasn't gotten full approval.

A big sigh escaped me, and I gripped the wheel a little tighter.

The warm glow of the carriage lights caught the Christmas wreaths in an angelic way. All the quaint shops were closed this early in the morning, but not Ben's Diner. When I drove by, I could see the regulars were already lined up like soldiers bellied up to the counter. Ben's baseball cap was turned around backwards like he'd always wore it. His mouth was already flapping while he went down the counter filling up all of the coffee mugs.

"I sure would like a cup of his coffee," I said to Duke and picked up my thermos I'd filled up with my coffee from home.

The old bean bag coffee holder slid off the floorboard hump when I got my coffee. I should've probably invested in a real cup holder for the old Wagoneer, but I couldn't bring myself to do it. This old Jeep was my Poppa's and many memories of me playing with the bean bag coffee holder were fond ones for me.

"It's not going to snow," I repeated to myself before I turned right into the Pump and Munch on the corner of East Oak and Main Street.

The Pump and Munch was the only gas station in downtown Cottonwood. There was a small market attached to the garage with two big steel doors and small windows across the top. Luke Jones was already hunkered under the hood of a car and looked up when my tires ran over the tube that dinged the bell inside.

He gave a slight wave to let me know he'd seen me and I waved back. Luke believed in the old way of things and coming out to pump the gas himself.

When I saw him coming out the door, I pulled down my

visor and took out the gas card that belonged to the sheriff's department.

"Mornin', Sheriff." Luke wiped his hands down the blue cover-alls he was wearing, which didn't make any sense because it appeared they were just as dirty as his hands. "You fillin' up to get the Jeep ready for the storm of the century?" he asked as we both saw his breath.

"Storm of the century?" I asked and pushed Duke away from my lap. He couldn't contain himself to his side of the front seat when my window was rolled down. "Just a little dusting."

Luke's arm plunged inside of the window as he reached across me to pat Duke. A stream of bitter air came with it.

"That's what all them meteorologist are calling it. Saying it's just like the blizzard of 1977." His chin lifted up and then down. "The way I figure it, I'm gonna be busy. People gonna come in here today to get gas for all their cars and generators." He pointed over to the side of his garage. "I've got plenty of gas cans on hand to sell. You need one?"

"Mark my word," I smiled and shook my head, "There's not going to be a storm of the century. Maybe a few flakes here and there, but they're always wrong."

"The Farmer's Almanac said so too." Luke's brows furrowed. He put his hands together and blew in them before he briskly rubbed them together. "Don't you got one?"

"Of course, I do." I took in a deep breath. "Doesn't everyone in Cottonwood?" I questioned under my breath.

Everyone in my small Southern town lived and died by the Farmer's Almanac. If you didn't get your seeds or crops planted by the time the black ink on the pages said, your crops weren't going to grow. But who was I to question it? I wasn't a farmer. Just a girl in love that wasn't going to let a few snowflakes keep her from meeting who could potentially be her future in-laws.

Just the thought of it made my stomach flip-flop and heart flutter.

"Filler' up?" He asked.

"Please," I said and rubbed my hands together. "And not because of the storm. I just need gas."

There was no denying that the temps were prime for a blizzard, but the sun was out and there was no way Poppa was going to let this happen. I looked up to the sky and said a little pray in my head.

"You're all set." He tapped the window sill. "What night are you and the gals coming by for *White Christmas* this week?"

Luke Jones and his wife, Vita, also owned the only community movie theater in Cottonwood. It was run in the basement of their house. They had popcorn, sweet treats, and drinks to purchase. He had a big pull-down screen that sometimes worked and sometimes didn't. On the days that it didn't want to pull down, he used a sheet screen that was actually three king sheets that Vita sewed together. Every year he ran the old movie, *White Christmas*, for three or four nights during the Christmas season. My best friends, Jolee Fischer and Tibbie Bell, and I had a yearly habit of making a girls' night out during Christmas that included our annual viewing of *White Christmas* at Luke's.

"Actually, I won't be coming. Finn invited me to Chicago to meet his family during the days you're showing the movie." The smile on my face got so big, I blushed. "We are going up a few days before Christmas so I'm going to miss all the fun festivities at the fairgrounds and everything." I planted a frown on my face for effect.

"Kenni," Luke gasped, his eyes grew big. "I knew you were

going out of town, but this'll be the first time that I can remember where you weren't in front row with a big popcorn sprinkled with chocolate and big coke."

"I know." I shrugged. "I'll have to start a new tradition with a New Year's movie."

"Who's going to run our town?" The line between his brows deepened.

"The state reserve is sending someone to run the joint. I don't anticipate anything going wrong," I said. "He'll be in the office today. So be nice if you see a stranger meandering around our parts."

It wasn't unusual for the town folk to give the riot act to any stranger in town that appeared to be gawking or a little too nosy. Gossip spread around our small town like wild fire and if I could make the temporary deputy comfortable before he got here, I was going to try. The last thing I needed when I was in Chicago was to get a call from Betty saying the people ran him out of town.

"What about the big blizzard? What if someone is trapped? Needs rescuing?" He asked.

It took everything in my power not to roll my eyes.

"Luke, mark my words, there's not going to be a big blizzard. They haven't gotten the weather right in years. Everything is going to be fine. I promise," I assured him, then crossed my heart and jerked the gear shift into drive. "Duke and I are off to do the rounds."

"Tell everyone you know to grab some milk, just in case. I've stocked up if Dixon's is out." He tapped the side of my Jeep before I took off.

There was no denying that it was going to be strange not being in Cottonwood during Christmas. I'd never not been here during Christmas. Even when I went off the college and joined the police academy, I came home every year. Change was good. At least that's what I was telling myself.

"Kenni, Kenni." Betty Murphy's voice came across the walkie-talkie loud and clear.

While I held on the steering wheel with one hand, I used the other to turn down the volume on the walkie-talkie strapped to my shoulder. It was the old way of communication, which Finn had tried desperately to get us to change, but it worked.

Like my Poppa always said, why try to fix something that's not broken?

"Go ahead," I said after I clicked the button on the side and crossed over York Street.

"Jilly Graves needs you to come to their house right away. Leighann didn't come home last night and it's not like her to do that." Betty Murphy was my dispatch operator at the department.

"Not like her to do that," I said sarcastically and looked over at Duke. "It was totally like her to not come home."

I reached up and clicked the button on the walkie-talkie.

"How long has Leighann been gone?" I asked, doing my civic duty.

"Since she left the Hunt Club dance last night." Betty clicked off.

"It's not even been twelve hours," I said to Duke. Leighann Graves had been giving her family fits for years by sneaking out. "She's probably at Manuel's after they made up from last night." I remembered how they'd gotten into that little tiff.

Duke's big brown eyes looked at me. His tongue was sticking out with a drip of slobber while he panted.

"Are you at the department?" I asked Betty when I noticed

the hands of the manual old-time clock on the dash said it was still thirty minutes until she was due to the office to start her job as dispatcher.

"Well, Jilly knew I wasn't in the office yet and so she called me at home. I rushed right on in here so I could get ahold of you." Betty was talking so fast, she was out of breath. "I knew you were probably off doing your rounds, and I would've called Finn, but he started his shift down at the Dixon's Foodtown ringing the bell for the kettle foundation this morning. You know, the thing you volunteered him for."

This was the time of year that I knew if the department didn't volunteer for anything, it'd come back and bite me in the you-know-what when it was election time. Sheriff was an elected position and it was hell enough trying to get the residents to vote in a female, hard enough now that I was here and under a microscope. Luckily, we'd just gotten through an election and I was safe for another four years.

"Alrighty. I'll run on over to the Graves's house, though I don't classify Leighann as missing and you know that until she's missing for a couple of days, we don't usually take report. She's an adult too." I figured it was another one of Sean Graves's ways of trying to keep control of his daughter.

Graves Towing and the Graves's house was on the north side of town past Lulu's Boutique. It wasn't like it took me long to get from the south edge of town to the north edge. Driving under a few stop lights and I had made it. Since I was already heading north on Main Street, it'd be quick.

Sean Graves was a third-generation family business owner and had kept up the company. The white clapboard farmhouse on the family farm was surrounded by black Kentucky post fencing. He took pride on how nice and neat he kept the property, as he should be. It was a beautiful farm.

The tow lot was full of cars that he'd repossessed or even took in as a junk, even sold some of the parts to customers. Behind a chain-link fence was the ever-mounting pile of a junk yard.

I drove up the driveway and around the back of the big farmhouse where the entrance was to their home. Their business was located behind the house and that's where you could see the generations of the Graves's hard work.

Sean and Jilly had lived off the property in a small home in town while Leighann was in school, but over the past few months, they'd moved back to the farm and focused more on the business. Especially since Leighann had decided not to go to college and to continue to work with the family business instead. At least that's what the word around town was. By that, I mean gossip.

The Sheriff's department used Graves's Towing a lot. We had no other choice. I didn't mind going out there to ease their minds. After all, they'd hung signs on their fence and voted for me in both elections.

Colored Christmas lights were strung across the gutters of their house. The few bushes on each side of the front door had those nets that were made out of white Christmas lights. They had a blow-up famous cartoon character in their front yard with a beer in his hand and a Santa hat on his head. That didn't shock me. It was a pretty typical characterization of Sean Graves. One of the good ole boys in Cottonwood.

I just shook my head and put the Jeep in park.

"Come on," I said to Duke and patted my leg. It wasn't unusual for him to be with me. My deputy and protector. He'd even received a medal for saving my life once and taking a bullet for me.

Duke jumped out my side and ran up to the bushes, leaving his mark on each one. I grabbed my police bag and shut the door. My bag was everything I needed when I went on a call or an investigation. No matter what type of call it was. It was easier to grab the whole thing than to get the notebook and pencil out.

"I'm guessing by the lack of the sheriff's light, my Leighann's disappearance isn't that important." Sean Graves stood at the door with bags under his eyes. He must've been watching for me.

"If there was someone out on the roads this early, I'd've used it, but I was lucky enough the roads were clear." I wasn't going to use the siren. I was positive that Leighann had just pulled one of her tricks again. "Which got me here quicker."

"Get on in here." He opened the door wide. When I took a step in, I could see Jilly sitting on the couch next to the stocked-up fire in the wood burning stove. There was a kettle on top with steam rolling out from the spout.

"Sheriff, would you like a cup of coffee?" She asked. There was a bit of fear in her that I'd not seen before when Leighann would disappear.

"That'd be great." I pointed to the chair. "May I?"

"Of course. Sean, go get Kenni a mug out of the cupboard. Can I get something for Duke?" She asked.

"No. He's fine." I pointed to the ground for Duke to take his command.

"Go on, Sean." Jilly shooed him to get me that coffee.

When I sat down, Duke laid down next to my feet. On the opposite side, I sat my bag down and unzipped it, taking out the notepad and paper.

While Jilly made sure I was comfortable, and Sean got my

coffee, I wrote down the date, time and purpose of the visit so I could transfer my notes into the computer when I got back into the office.

"I got a call from Betty saying that Leighann is missing." I took the cup and nodded a thank you. "Why do you think this is different than any other time?" I asked.

"This." Jilly held up a cell phone. "This is Leighann's. You and I both know that these kids today don't put their phones down. Especially her. She's on this thing twenty-four seven."

"I was beginning to think it'd attached to her skin she never puts it down." Sean offered me creamer and I held my hand up declining.

I sat the coffee on the small table next to me and took a vested interest because they did have a point, though I wasn't thoroughly convinced Leighann was actually missing.

"We all know that the past is a proven history that Leighann has left here before." I reminded them of all the calls before Leighann was of legal age.

"Yes. But like I said, this is her phone and she never left without it in the past." Jilly eased herself to sit on the edge of the couch. Her hands clasped and tucked in between her knees.

"Is the phone still in your name? Do you pay the bill?" I asked and both of them nodded.

"Is it possible that she and Manuel got a phone in her name?" I asked again. "Maybe cutting some ties with you guys now that she's legally able to leave?"

"No. Both of their phones are owned by the company. We've accepted that she's out of high school and an adult. She's going to keep dating that boy no matter what we say." Sean seethed. Apparently, no matter what he told me, he'd not accepted their relationship and maybe not at any age.

Jilly leaned over and touched him to calm him down.

"We are open to the fact that she loves him, and we will train him and her to take over our business when we retire," Jilly said. "Just like your parents did for us."

"I want better for her." Sean jerked away from Jilly and stood up. He ran his hand through his hair and paced back and forth. "You and I have a hard enough time making ends meet. What's going to happen when we retire? They aren't as hardworking as us."

"This is the problem." Jilly's voice rose and octave. "You don't give them a chance to even try to grow up."

"Back to the cell phone." I had to reel them in. "Have you talked to Manuel this morning? Is she with him?"

"No. I mean yes." He waved his hand in the air. "She's not with him. And yes, we've talked to him. That's what worries me." Jilly said, "Sean and I left the dance last night before they did."

That I remembered.

"Manuel said there was some sort of argument. She and Manuel were leaving. She'd met him at the dance because he was on a call for us to pull in a repo. When they were leaving the dance, she threw the phone at him as she yelled that she didn't want him to call her and jumped in her car. She took off. He said he drove off after her, but she was going so fast that he couldn't keep up with her." A look of worry set deep in Jilly's eyes.

"He hasn't seen her since?" I asked.

"No. And that's not like her. You know just as much as we do the trouble we've had keeping her away from him even when they did fight. And they've had some doozies." Jilly looked at Sean. "That's why we tried to discourage them from dating. They have these big, blow up fights that are bad now. I can only imagine what would happen if they got married."

"Has Manuel ever hit Leighann?" I asked only because I wanted to get a complete picture of the type of relationship they'd had.

"We don't know. Leighann would never confess to anything. She says that they love each other so much that they fight." She scoffed, "Who ever heard alike?"

"Do you believe him when he says he's not seen her?" I questioned, keeping in mind that their opinion of him was a bit skewed.

"We don't know what to believe. After she graduated, we sat down with her and told her that we approved of her relationship. She didn't have to go to college and she could learn the business. She was pleased with that. When she and Manuel started working together every day, side by side, we noticed she'd gotten a little more distanced from him. Last year, she'd jump in the cab of the tow truck and go all day long when she was off a day from school. Now we have to beg her to go help him." Sean's lips pulled in and snugged up against his teeth. "I feel like something is wrong. I don't know if he had anything to do with it, but I can't find her. After he showed up here with this phone and said she never came to his house, he got worried and came here to see if she'd come home."

"We checked her phone. There's no unusual activity or calls and even her text messages are fine." Jilly sucked in a deep breath.

"Can I take her phone with me?" I asked. They readily handed it over to me. "If we can't find Leighann, which I'm sure we will, I can subpoena the records of the phone. Last ping. Those types of things. Is there any particular place she goes when she's upset or angry that you might know about?"

"She and Manuel liked to go down to the river over at

Chimney Rock, but I drove over there this morning after Manuel had come by. Granted, it was dark out, but I didn't see her car." Sean frowned. "I asked Manuel about Chimney Rock and he said that he didn't have plans to go there with her either."

"I'll go speak to Manuel. I also witnessed that argument last night. I even talked to them. There were a few other kids standing around. I'll go see the other kids involved. In the meantime," I put my note pad and Leighann's phone back in my bag. I pushed myself up to stand. Duke jumped up and trotted over to their door. "If you do hear from her, please call my cell immediately."

I took a business card with my cell phone printed on it and handed it to Sean.

"Thank you, Kenni." Sean walked me to the door. "If anyone can talk to Manuel and figure out what he might be hiding, it's you."

"I'll be in touch." I nodded and patted my leg for Duke to follow.

"You've got my cell number, right?" He questioned as I walked towards my Jeep.

"I sure do." I opened the door and Duke jumped in.

"Good. That big winter storm is coming, and I imagine I'll be out in it pulling out idiots who get out in that stuff. Do you have an emergency kit in your Jeep?" He asked and walked up to the driver's door.

"I've got what I need," I assured him.

"Everyone needs an emergency kit in their car at all times. I made sure Jilly has one and Leighann has one in her car. So if Leighann's in some sort of emergency right now," his voice cracked, "I know she's got food, water and first aid kit." He sniffed. "I even got her a kit from Lulu's boutique with her initials on it." He let out a little laugh. "Leighann is so girly. She loves all that initial stuff."

"I'm sure we'll find her," I assured him. My words met his blank face.

"Nonetheless, be careful in the storm." He slammed the door.

"There's not going to be a winter storm," I confidently yelled back to their front door.

Chapter Three

If I was going to drive out to the Liberty house, I figured I was going to need to get a fresh, hot coffee because just like Manuel, his mother wasn't one to mess with. Juanita Liberty let people know that Manuel was to go to college on a football scholarship. She didn't hold back when Manuel had told them he wasn't going to go to college, turning down the scholarship and staying in Cottonwood. It was a dispatch call that I dreaded and could still feel that sick gut feeling.

The call had actually come from Jonathan, Manuel's brother. Juanita had gotten Manuel in a choke hold, demanding she wasn't going to let go until he signed the scholarship, but Manuel insisted he wasn't going. It took a while for me to pry her hands from around the poor kid, but it did end peacefully.

Heading south, on my way back into town, I took a right next to Lulu's Boutique. Duke danced back and forth between the front seat and back seat of the Wagoneer in delight.

The boutique was a really old, small, yellow clapboard house that Lulu McClain had turned into a cozy knick-knack shop that sold local arts, candles, some clothing items and accessories for the home. In the back she'd host different arts and crafts for the various groups, like knitting, pottery, crocheting, and whatever else the Auxilary Women could find to fill their days and nights.

It wasn't the boutique that Duke was so excited to see, it was Jolee Fischer's food truck, On the Run. Jolee pulled the truck up to the curb next to Lulu's every morning so she could caffeinate all the Cottonwood people who got up early. The food she cooked and served was straight homecookin' that made our mouths water. Duke was a recipient of some of her treats and his tail nearly knocked me over as he jumped out of the Jeep after I opened the door. This was why I knew he'd be just fine while I was gone to Chicago.

It was too cold to eat outside, and Jolee knew when she opened the food truck that everyone needed a place to commune if they wanted to. Lulu and Jolee had made an agreement that Lulu would open the craft room in the back of the boutique for people to eat and enjoy. Cottonwood was about community and being together.

"Kenni, really?" Lulu came out of nowhere and wiped her hand across the front pocket of my brown sheriff's jacket. "You could use a little monogram on this to make it pop a little. Or make it a little more feminine."

She pulled away and her fingernails racked the edge of her short, twiggy styled black hair. There was some jingling going on under the faux fur coat she had snuggled around her. No doubt the jingling was the armful of bangles she had from her wrist to her elbow.

"Lulu, it's monogramed with the sheriff's symbol." My eyes lowered, "Have you been talking to Mama?" I asked.

"Have I?" She squealed with delight. "I just have to show you that fur coat she's going to look fabulous in when she's sitting on the back of a fancy car in a parade."

"Lulu, you aren't feeding Mama a line of bullarky about this silly notion of her wanting to run for Snow Queen, are you?" I gave her a sideways look.

"Well, she mentioned something about you going to Chicago and she's got to have something to fill up her broken heart. But I did tell her that you'd be a beautiful bride. If you insist on going, we would like you to have something come out of it. After all," She cozied up to me, "a fall wedding in Cottonwood is beautiful." Her nails dug into me.

"You and my Mama can get any notion of me getting engaged while I'm in Chicago out of your head." Though the image of me being Finn's bride might've popped in my head a time or two, it wasn't something I figured on right now.

Come on? What girl didn't start dreaming of her wedding at age three?

Lulu let out a long sigh.

"Fancy nails you got there." I pulled her hand away from my arm and noticed the red and gold tips with a smidgen of glitter on them. "Shimmery."

"Oh honey, I'm one of Tina Bower's Guinea pigs down at Tiny Tina's." She curled her nose. "All that shines makes my heart sing."

"It's cold. I'm going to grab a coffee." I patted her on the back. "You're dressed for Antarctica."

"I'm getting out all my furs due to the storm of the century coming." She shimmied proudly and ran her hand down the front of her coat with a twinkle in her eye. "Not just your Mama wants one of my fine furs."

"Don't tell me that you're believing this weather forecast?" I questioned because Lulu McClain was one that didn't let anyone pull the wool over her eyes. "Of all people in this town, I didn't figure you'd fall for it."

"Honey," her Southern accent made her response so much more charming, "I'll give it to you that the weather people on the television are probably about ninety-nine percent wrong, but I do believe with the way the clouds are shifting and the wind is breezing, they might've gotten that one percent right this time." She shivered and wiggled her shoulders. "Can't you feel it?"

"Nope. Not one bit." I shrugged and wasn't about to give into the fact that she had her faith in the one percent.

"Put your nose in the air and smell it." She jutted her chin out and up, taking the biggest inhale. "Agggghhhhhh," she released it. "I can smell it and I can see it." She dragged her hands out in front of her. "The freshly fallen snow that blankets Cottonwood in all its sparkling splendor. The real thick snow that the kiddos can pack into the tallest snowmen you've ever seen." She elbowed me. "We haven't had a snow like that since you were a youngin'."

"I remember." It wasn't a fond memory either. "Mama decided she needed to go to Dixon's Foodtown when Daddy told her not to. She threw me in the back of the family station wagon and backed out of the driveway and before she even got going the wagon slid back and hit a fire hydrant."

Lulu's brows furrowed.

"That's when Graves's Tow company came and got us out. I can hear daddy now," I continued in my best dad voice, "'Viv, I told you not to go out in this stuff, but you had to be nosy.' Mama said, 'no I wanted to get bread.' Dad said back to her that she was wanting to make sure she wasn't missing out on any gossip in the baking aisle. Then they fought over the big bill from Graves's towing. Right here at Christmas time." I shook my head. "I'm hoping the weather is still ninety-nine percent wrong."

"We'll see," Lulu ho-hummed and gave me a wink as she walked away.

The line to the front of On the Run food truck was about five people deep. Each one greeted me with the typical nod and "mornin' sheriff". Of course, I was kind and asked how they were doing. Before I knew it, I'd gotten caught up on their lives and I made sure to ask them if they'd seen Leighann Graves. No one had and before you knew it, I was up to the front of the line where Jolee had my coffee poured and ready to go.

"You haven't seen Leighann Graves around have you?" I asked.

Not that I'd expected Jolee to say yes or even that Leighann had stopped by the food truck. No stone unturned was the motto I liked to live by and you just never knew.

"I haven't. I don't even remember her ever coming here, but not that she wouldn't today. It's been a weird morning." Jolee leaned over and out the window of the food truck. She turned her head right and left. "None of my regulars are here. I swear it's this whole snow thing. Damn storm of the century."

"There's not going to be a storm." I looked at her up under my brows. "You're my best friend. You can at least agree with me."

"Unn-hun, no way." She shook her head. "You're trying to bail out on our annual *White Christmas* girl's night. I don't want you leaving me for Christmas. Who cares about you leaving your Mama behind. It's me you're leaving behind."

"Whatever. You've got Ben," I said.

She wasn't fooling me any, though she'd never bailed on a girlfriend night since she started dating Ben Harrison.

"Anyways, if you see Leighann let me know. She didn't

come home last night after she got into that fight with Manuel at the dance. She'll turn up." I was sure of it.

"I'm sure she will." Jolee's eyes moved past me and onto the next customer.

"Let's go, Duke," I called after my trusty sidekick.

There was just something about going to see someone early in the morning. It always felt like an intrusion. Was I waking them up? Catching them at a bad time? Were they going to work? Still in their pjs?"

As the sheriff, I had to put those feelings and silly notions aside and rely on intuition when I got there. I'd have Duke and my other trusty sidekick, my pistol.

The Libertys lived on the outskirts of the south side of town. I had to take interstate sixty-eight and take a left on Keene Road. Not that Keene was a bad area to live in, it was just a small community that stuck together. They were a tight-knit group of neighbors. The houses needed a lot of work, but they didn't care. Most days you'd drive through Keene and everyone would be outside talking to the neighbors.

The Libertys' home was a small brick home with a poured concrete front porch slab. The Christmas lights hung around the door were barren and missing a couple of twinkles every couple of bulbs. The doorbell hung out from the brick and barely hung on by the wires that attached it. I knocked a few times since getting electrocuted wasn't on my Christmas list.

"What you want?" Juanita Liberty stood at the door. Her massive head of black hair was piled up on the top of her head and falling down on the sides. There were bags underneath her eyes.

"Sheriff," Manual pushed past his Mama and out the front door. Beka Durst, Angela's daughter was standing in the background with Juanita's other son, Jonathan. Manuel tugged on his Cottonwood high school sweat shirt. "Did you go look for Leighann?"

"Leighann?" Juanita's nose turned up like she smelled a fart. "What's she done now? Not that getting you to quit football and stay in this god-forsaken town your whole life after I uprooted our family to give you a better life was enough."

"Leighann Graves?" Beka asked with a concerned look. "Is she okay?"

"Who cares?" Juanita said over her shoulder.

"Don't mind her." Manual pulled the door shut behind him with Juanita still fussing about how much she disliked Leighann to Beka and Jonathon.

This was the exact reason I didn't want to come here this morning, but I was elected to do a job.

"I'm guessing you haven't seen her?" I asked. By the looks of him, he'd been up all night.

"No. And it's unlike her when we have a fight for her not to come running back or at least give me more of a piece of her mind until we make up." He blinked his big brown eyes. His lips turned down. "I love her, sheriff, I do."

"I'm not sure what your fight was about last night, but publicly fighting or fighting at all wasn't the brightest idea." It was my opportunity to mother him a smidgen since it appeared his mother hadn't. "What was the fight about?" I asked.

"Just stuff. Mean girl stuff." He shrugged.

"Your Mama really doesn't like Leighann?" I asked and nodded towards the only front window where Juanita was watching us and yammering on a mile a minute about what I could guess was still Leighann.

"She's mad that I've decided to stay here in Cottonwood

and not go play college football, but that's not Leighann's fault. Leighann told me to go. Encouraged me. But I just don't want to. Even her parents have finally gotten to the point where they can tolerate me." He gave a weak smile. "Now this," he swallowed hard and choked back the lump that seemed to have gotten in his throat.

"Do you have any idea where she might've gone?" I gave suggestions only to get head shakes. "Friends? Old flame? Family member?"

"None of those that I know of. I went through her phone before I gave it to her parents to see if she got any calls, but she didn't. No messages. Me and her are inseparable." He let out a long sigh.

"What about Chimney Rock?" I asked, wondering if she were sitting down there right now with her heat on, Christmas tunes cranked and just waiting them out for a few hours.

"No. We always made plans to go down there, but not during the winter and certainly not with this big blizzard coming." His words made me glare at him.

There's not going to be a blizzard, were the words that formed a bitter taste in my mouth, but instead of saying them out loud, I said, "Sean did say that she'd stopped going on tow runs with you." Not that I suspected he knew where she was, but it would give an indication if she was mad and staying away for a little. "And it's not unlike her to not to come home."

"When she didn't come home, she was with me." He was getting fidgety. "We'd tell them if she wasn't coming home so they wouldn't worry, even though we didn't have to anymore since she is an adult."

"There wasn't a place that the two of you went that you're not remembering?" I asked.

"No. No. No." He looked down and shuffled his feet. "As for work, just recently she started to say that it wasn't good for us to work together all the time. I didn't know what that meant. She said something about how she didn't want us to be like her parents. I didn't know what that meant either. I figured her parents got in a fight and her mom said something about putting up with Sean all her life, like she always throws that in his face and Leighann would open up when she was ready to." He paused, "Maybe she's getting sick of me," his voice cracked.

"If you remember anything or any place she might've gone, please call me. Or stop by the station." I suggested.

He clearly needed someone to lean on, but I wasn't a therapist. I barely got my own relationship going a year or so ago, no way could I help out anyone else.

"You better be careful out there, Sheriff," he said. "The news just said that storm of the century is headed right towards us."

"I'll be fine," I smiled but silently cursed the weather person, "I can guarantee that storm will shift right before it's due to hit and we won't see nary a flake."

"Huh." Manuel scratched his head. "You're the authority, I guess you should know."

"Let me know if you hear from Leighann." I tugged the Wagoneer door open a little harder than normal. The last time I had to do that was when my Poppa had come to get me during that snow storm Lulu had mentioned earlier.

Poppa told me to tug because the chill lingering in the air made the old Wagoneer door stick a little. He also told me that's how he knew the storm was coming.

"Good boy," I ran my hand down Duke because he stayed on his side of the Jeep when I got in and didn't try to jump out.

I looked up to the sky. My jaw tensed.

"Okay," I said my prayer out loud, "Poppa, if you can hear me, right now is the time." Most times, I'd summon him when I was trying to solve a murder and he'd conveniently disappear. This time I needed that storm to shift. "Blow on that storm. Don't let that storm hit here."

Duke leaned over and gave me a big lick across my cheek, bringing me back to my senses.

"You're right." I laughed. "I'm acting nuts. There's not a storm coming," I assured myself.

If only I believed myself.

Chapter Four

"Something smells good today." I stepped into Cowboy's Catfish after parking the Wagoneer in front of the restaurant on Main Street. "I could smell it as soon as I got out of my car." I patted my stomach.

"Mornin' Sheriff," Bartleby Fry, owner of Cowboy's Catfish, was busy wiping off one of the tables next to the door. "That'll be the special this mornin'. Kentucky round steak and scrambled eggs." He threw the damp cloth over his shoulder and reached down to pat Duke. "I've got you something special."

"Just a nibble," I warned Bartleby. "We are both getting fat with all this cooking." I patted my stomach and teased on my way back to the department. Though I do love me some Kentucky round steak and eggs, which was just a fancy name for fried bologna. "You send Duke back to the department when he starts to get on your nerves."

The back room in Cowboy's Catfish restaurant was where the Cottonwood Sheriff's department was located. To some that might be strange, but not for a small town in Kentucky. After all, we had a movie theatre in Luke Jones's basement along with the town hall meetings. Our entire town seemed weird, but it was quaint to us.

"Good morning," I chirped when I walked into the office with my cup of coffee in one hand and my bag in the other.

There was a man lounging in Finn's chair. He looked super comfortable all leaned back with his hands folded together across his belly.

"Hi there," I greeted him personally.

"Sheriff Kenni Lowry, State Reserve Office Scott Lee." Betty Murphy tugged one of her pink curlers out of her hair.

"Sheriff?" Scott looked funny at me. It was the whole girl sheriff thing that threw men off.

"Nice to meet you Officer Lee. We are grateful you're here." I shook his hand. "I'm really excited to get some much-needed time off."

"I'm happy to be here." He pulled off his big round State Reserve hat that looked a little like the Boris Badenov, in *Rocky and Bullwinkle*. "I'm ready to serve the people of Cottonwood, which I hear is about to be under a few feet of snow."

"Shhhh," Betty looked at him and slowly shook her head. "Don't mention snow in front of her," Betty warned him.

"Right!" I snapped my fingers at Betty. "You know why? There's not going to be any snow." I assured him. "If there was any chance of that, then I wouldn't need you because I'd be snowed in from my trip and that's not going to happen." I looked at Betty. Her lips were tucked in between her teeth. "Right, Betty?"

"Right, Sheriff." She smiled and nodded. The remaining curlers flipped and flopped with each nod.

"What did you find out about Leighann Graves?" Betty asked.

"I found out that she didn't come home, and Juanita Liberty hates her as much as the Graves hate her boy." I sat my bag on my desk and took a long drink of coffee before I walked over to the closet next to our only cell in the room. "What size are you, Scott?"

"Medium shirt, size thirty-one thirty-two pants," he said and walked over to me.

"I'm sure she's mad. We can put an APB out on her car. I got her license plate number written down on my notepad." I handed Scott his Cottonwood Sheriff's uniform to use while he was there. "I know it's not as flattering as your reserve blues, but brown is all we got and stands for a lot around here."

"No problem." He looked around. "The restroom to change?"

"Right on through the door." I gestured towards the restaurant. "We use the same bathroom as the restaurant."

There was a perplexed look on his face. He didn't say a word.

"Give me the juice on Leighann Graves," Betty begged and jumped right on in after the door shut behind Scott. "Don't leave a single thing out."

She rested the back end of her house dress on the edge of her desk. Heaven help us if Betty Murphy ever came to the office in the sheriff uniforms we've given her.

"There's nothing more than I told you. The people that Leighann hangs around haven't heard from her. I did get her cell phone and I'm going to sit down here and go through it. In the meantime," I unzipped my bag and took out my notebook. "Take this license number and run it. Put out an APB. See if she's been stopped by any neighboring towns and go ahead and put out a statewide Amber alert on her. Call the hospitals. You know the drill." I scribbled the number down.

"You do think she's missing?" Betty took the sticky note

from me.

"Why do you think that?" I asked.

"This is against your twenty-four-hour rule." She stared at me from over top of her glasses.

"I just want to make sure everything is nice and tidy before I head out of town next week. That means Leighann Graves at home in her bed when Santa comes to town," I assured her.

Not that Leighann was a child. She was eighteen and she could do whatever darn well she pleased, but this wasn't normal circumstances. I was going to Chicago. A rare occasion for a sheriff in a department of three employees to take off and I'd been planning it for months. A snippy, mad teenager in love wasn't going to ruin my plans.

"Sheriff's department." I grabbed the phone before Betty could because I wanted her to get that alert out. "This is the sheriff," I assured the person on the other end of the line.

"Kenni, it's Doolittle Bowman. I was pulling my boat out of the river because you know that big storm is about to hit and it's not good for a boat to be in frozen water and under snow," she said.

Doolittle Bowman was head of the town council.

If there was a complaint in town or a business mishap, people called and filed those complaints with Doolittle. She also led the town meetings in Luke's basement. She took pride in banging her gavel.

"What is it that you called about, Doolittle?" I asked, trying to figure out what she wanted.

"I was pulling out my boat and saw what looks like one of them Toyota four-doors sticking ass-end out of the water. I think that's strange." She wasn't one to worry about how she said things or even offended people.

"That is odd." I grabbed a pen and the sticky note. "Where was this?" I asked.

"Down at the Chimney Rock boat dock right where you put in and pull out." She referred to the public boat ramp that local boaters used to put their boats in the Kentucky River, which bordered Cottonwood.

"I'm on my way." I hung up the phone. "What did I write down about Leighann's make and model of the car?" I held my breath hoping it wasn't Leighann's car.

"Nissan or something." After those words left her mouth, my heart went back to beating since Doolittle said it was a Toyota. "Who was that?"

"It was Doolittle. She said that there's a car submerged in the river." I grabbed my cell phone. "Do you mind giving Scott a tour of the place?"

"What's there to tour?" She pointed. "That's your desk." She patted her desk. "This is mine." She pointed again. "That over there is Finn's desk."

"You know what I mean." I glared at her. "All the papers he'll need if he gets called out and how to work the fax. The schedule we keep. Like check the messages in the morning. Call to see if there were any dispatches overnight."

Since it was a two man...errr...one man, one woman's office, and Betty on dispatch during the day, we didn't have a night dispatch. Unless you counted all the residents calling my cell phone, we used Clay's Ferry, the neighboring town's, dispatch service.

Clay's Ferry was a little bigger than Cottonwood, so they had a much larger department. We traded off favors every once in a while, and I offered my services where I could. It was the neighborly thing to do.

"Take care of Duke for me," I called out on my way back through the restaurant where Duke was still sitting patiently next to Bartleby while he cooked over the hot grill.

Once I got into the Jeep and headed east of town on Sulphur Well Road towards the river, I grabbed my cell and told my phone to call Sean Graves. I was going to need a tow truck and maybe some work would be something he needed to get out of his house.

"Did you find her?" Sean answered the phone without even saying hello.

"I was hoping I'd call and she was home." I was having an inner struggle on whether to ask him to come or get the tow company from Clay's Ferry to meet me there. I pulled to a stop at the four-way stop sign where I needed to take a right on the curvy country road leading me straight to the boat dock. Cell service was spotty.

"No. Not a word." His voice faded off. "I'm trying to work, but I just can't concentrate. Did you talk to Manuel?"

"Yes. He hasn't seen her nor has his family," I said. "I've got a job if you're up to it. Might be good for you to get out of the house."

I would let him to decide. When he gave me the go-ahead, I proceeded and told him to meet me at Chimney Rock put in. He said he was on his way and it'd be a much-needed distraction for him.

"Chimney Rock?" He questioned with a nervous tone. "Do you think?"

"Doolittle didn't describe Leighann's car," I said and tried to give him some peace of mind. "I just thought maybe I'd call you and get you out of the house."

"I forgot how cold these winter storms make these doors

stick." My Poppa's ghost sat in the passenger seat, vigorously rubbing his hands together.

I slammed the breaks of the Wagoneer, bringing it to a screeching halt.

Chapter Five

"I'm guessing you aren't here to tell me that you've taken care of my little request about the storm of the century?" I asked and tried to hide my fear I was feeling inside my gut.

Seeing Poppa's ghost was no big deal, I'd gotten used to it. The reason I was nervous about seeing his ghost was the fear. The only time the ghost of my Poppa came to see me was when there was a murder in Cottonwood. Something I'd come to realize after the first murder that'd happened in Cottonwood during my second year of my elected four-year term.

Long story short, my Poppa and I figured out that he was my ghost deputy during a major crime. All the years before, his ghost was running around scaring off any would-be criminals which made Cottonwood crime free under my watch, until there just so happened to be two crimes going on at once. Ghost or not, he couldn't be in two places at once. Here he was.

"Nope. Not here for the weather." Slowly he shook his head. "Trust me when I'm going to tell you that it got on my nerves listening to you beg me to change Mother Nature's mind. She's just like any other woman. When her mind is set, it's set."

His words or presences didn't bring me any comfort at this particular time.

I gulped. I shook my hands in the air to keep them from tremoring before I grabbed the steering wheel. I wasn't sure how long I was there, but I know it was long enough for Sean Graves to pull up to the four-way stop, beep, and startle me.

I glanced in the rear-view and saw his face, then I slid my gaze over to Poppa. His chin drew an imaginary line up and then down. I closed my eyes, took a deep breath and reminded myself that I had a job to do and remain calm.

I jumped when there was a knock on my driver's side window.

"You okay? Do I need to tow you?" Sean tried to joke, though I knew his heart was worried, and soon to be broken.

I manually rolled the window down.

"Actually," I was taken off guard with the sudden puffs of air smoke coming from my mouth as the air mingled with my words. "I don't need you after all. False alarm. No car."

No way was I going to take the chance that the car was Leighann's and Doolittle didn't know what she was talking about. Who didn't know the Toyota symbol verses a Nissan?

Sean looked at me. His jaw tensed. It was as if he could read my mind. He stormed back to his tow truck. I jumped out of the Jeep and put my hands out in front of me as he barreled the big truck around my Jeep and towards me.

"Sean. Don't go. Sean. Do not go." I begged him as he went around me, not giving two-cents if he was going to hit me.

When I realized he wasn't going to stop, I jumped back into the Wagoneer.

"Damn, damn, damn." I reached under the seat and pulled out the old red police beacon. I licked the suction cup and stuck my hand out the window, sticking the siren on top of the roof. My finger glided over the switch and turned on the siren.

The red siren circled in the air, giving its shadow to the empty-leaved trees that lined the old road. I passed the tow truck once I'd caught up with him. There was no way I was going to let him get there before me.

"Tell me," I urged my Poppa. "Tell me what's going on."

"I think you already know why I'm here. I done told you it wasn't about the weather." He wasn't one to mix words when it came to official sheriff business. When I glanced over at him as I drove on the straightaway before I took the sharp curve, his eyes were dark, struck with fear. "I hate to see the demise of any young person."

My eyes filled with tears as I tried to focus back on the road. I reached up to my walkie-talkie and pushed in the button.

"Betty, can you send Deputy Lee to Chimney Rock." I knew I couldn't send for Finn. At least not until his volunteer shift at Dixon's Foodtown was over. There wasn't nothing wrong with throwing Scott right on into the frying pan.

"Sure. Is everything alright?" she asked back.

"I don't think so. I think we've found Leighann Graves's car," I said. The words left a chilly trail up my spine.

I knew it wasn't just the car that was found since Poppa was here, but I couldn't let the cat out of the bag until the facts were presented.

See, only me, Duke and Poppa knew about Poppa. Not even Finn. Though it was getting harder and harder to hide how it was that I knew clues before those clues were even discovered. That didn't matter now. What mattered now was figuring out who did this to Leighann Graves.

"Oh Gawd, Kenni," Betty's voice quivered. "Do you think she's...um..."

"I don't know if she's in there or not." That wasn't a lie. The fact was that Poppa was here which meant Leighann had been murdered. The bigger question was where was her body? "I'll let you know as soon as we get the car pulled out of the water."

"You don't sound so confident." Betty couldn't have been more correct.

"I called Sean Graves to come pull the car out before I realized who the car belonged to," my voice trailed off when I saw Doolittle Bowman in the distance next to her big Dually truck and her boat hitched up to the back. "I'll call you back. Send Max," I reiterated before I got off the phone.

"Well," Poppa rubbed his hands together, "Let's get to it."

Poppa loved a good crime to solve. He was the reason I went into the academy. I'd spent many days and nights in this same Wagoneer riding around with him on calls. Murders were rare in Cottonwood, so it was mainly neighborly disputes over religion or opinions. Poppa would tell these people the same thing, "opinions are like assholes. Everybody has one. Just respect each other."

I wish it was as easy as that nowadays.

"Doolittle," I greeted her when I got out of the car.

"Sheriff," She pushed her glasses back up on the bridge of her nose. The knit stocking cap was tugged over her short hair. "Right on over there."

Without me having to even look, I knew Sean had pulled up when I heard a door slam followed up by stomping footsteps.

The gravel from the boat ramp spit up under my brown sheriff shoes with each hurried step. On each side of the ramp was a wooded area with tall trees that were barren of their leaves. The Kentucky Bluegrass had long gone into hibernation and would soon flourish in the spring as the limestone underneath warmed the earth's surface.

I walked into the wooded area to get down to the river bank a little more. By the looks of the river banks, it appeared the small SUV had drifted to the right once it went into the river and dragged down the banks. It also looked as though it went top heavy as it dragged along the shoreline, getting the nose stuck in the mud underneath the water. The only thing visible was the back window and tail lights and the fact it was red. The license plate was the exact match to Leighann's that Jilly and Sean had given me earlier.

"Oh my god, my baby!" Sean screamed and ran past me, confirming my worst fears. It was definitely Leighann's car.

"Sean!" I screamed at the top of my lungs before he could do anything stupid. I grabbed his arm and dug my nails into it. "Don't!"

"Get my baby out of there," he seethed through his gritted teeth. His finger jutted towards the river.

Out of the corner of my eye, I saw Poppa walk down into the water and disappear.

"We don't know she's in there. It could just be her car," I said in a steady voice. I tried to talk to him calmly so he'd settle down a little bit, though I knew it was probably hoping for too much. "If there's some evidence in the car or on the car and you jump in, I won't be able to use it to help find her."

"You think there's hope?" His eyes burned with tears.

"I think you need to let me do my job." I let go of him when I felt like he was a little more together. "Now, if you don't think you can pull..." I stopped and had to keep my composure when Poppa came out of the water. His face said it all. "Listen," I tried to turn Sean around so he'd stop staring at the backend of the car. "I'm going to call S&S Auto from Clay's Ferry."

"Why would you do that when I'm right here and can get it

out?" He got unglued and started to pace back and forth.

"Because of this." I pointed out his behavior. "You are rightfully so upset. I need this to be pulled out with no emotions attached to it whatsoever. That means you need to let me do my job and what I think is best. And." I gave him a firm look and took a deep breath. "And, if she is in there, I can't have the scene tainted until it's processed."

About that time, Scott pulled up in his car and got out.

"Who the hell is that?" Sean asked with disgust.

"This is Officer Lee, Scott Lee. He's with the state reserve and will be here during Christmas." I knew Sean wasn't comprehending anything I was saying, but I had to go through the motions. "He's going to talk to you while I make that call to S&S."

Sean nodded and sat down on the cold earth.

"Why don't you come sit in my car," Scott suggested to Sean. "I've got a nice hot cup of coffee from Cowboy's Catfish you can sip on to keep you warm until we get this all straightened out."

"I'll be a yellow-bellied-sap-sucker," Poppa eyeballed Scott and repeated one of his favorite phrases that meant he was in shock. "This here feller is a perfect fit for your department. He knows how to talk to everyone."

I ignored Poppa until I took a few steps towards the car and away from the other people so I could ask him some questions.

"What did you see in the car?" I asked under my breath.

"She's in there. Or someone is in there. Long hair floating around the face." The edges of Poppa's lips turned down. "I'm figuring it's the Graves girl."

I gulped. The stinging pain of tears crept up in the back of my nose and rested in my tear ducts as I tried to keep them from coming out.

"Kenni!" I jerked around when I heard Finn's voice. He hurried towards me. Poppa disappeared. "Why didn't you call me? I had to find out from Toots Buford at Dixon's when she came in for her shift. She asked me what happened because she heard it on police scanner."

"That's exactly how they all found out." I gestured to all the cars that were showing up and parking along the outskirts of the Chimney Rock boat dock.

"Doesn't take long around here." Finn's brows rose when he looked over at Scott and Sean. "Is it the Graves's girl car?"

"Afraid so." I put my finger up and clicked the walkie-talkie.

"Go ahead, Sheriff," Betty's voice rang out in the quiet and echoed off the cliffs that surrounded the river. I rolled the volume down.

"Betty, can you call S&S Auto in Clay's Ferry to come here?" It wasn't necessarily a question, but she agreed and clicked off. "I had no clue it was her when I asked Sean to come pull it out. I figured it would be good for him to work and get Leighann off his mind."

"Let's hope she's not in there." Finn looked at me through some very optimistic eyes. "What? You look funny. You think she's in there, don't you?"

"It doesn't look good. That's all," I stated. "No one has seen her. She's not tried to get to her phone."

Over the next twenty minutes as we waited on the tow company to get there, more and more citizens showed up. Most of them were out of their cars and had gathered at the top of the ramp. Sean had gotten out of the car and joined them. I left it up to him to give them any updates he found necessary.

Finn and I both got out the police tape and began to mark

off the property where we felt was enough to preserve any sort of evidence. I made sure it was far away from the view of the car because I didn't want the public to see us tow it out.

We still needed to scour the ground. I was praying for us to find something, but I didn't know what. I'd gotten the camera out of my bag and took photos of the ramp, though Doolittle Bowman's pull out had brought a lot of the lake water with it, washing away any evidence left from Leighann's car.

The wind had picked up and I zipped up my coat.

"Looks like it's moving in." Poppa bounced on his toes and looked up to the sky. "Wee-doggie it's gonna be a good one."

"Do you see something?" Finn asked.

In a normal relationship, I'd been thrilled my boyfriend was watching my every move, but with my Poppa's ghost here, I had to be more diligent of my reaction to him.

"Nothing." I stuck my hands in my pockets. "It's getting windy." I glared at Poppa, giving him the unspoken gesture to skit out of here. "I'm not sure if it's the cold chill sending shivers up my legs or what we might find in that car."

"Sheriff, do you have a statement for the Cottonwood Chronicle?" Edna Easterly asked with her handheld tape recorder held over the police tape.

The brown fedora was perched on top of her head. The feather waving in the gust of wind. The index card that had REPORTER written in Sharpie was barely dangling on the hat. She had on her fishing vest with all the pockets over top of her winter coat. She filled the pockets with all her reporter stuff.

"People want to know if it's Leighann Graves and if it is, is it foul play?" She yelled out questions. "Is her own dad going to pull out her car? I heard from an unnamed source that she and Manuel Liberty were in a fight last night. Do you think he did something to her? You were seen at the Liberty house this morning, why were you there?"

"Hi, Edna." I could feel the tension starting to build above my brows. I rubbed my forehead on my way over to talk to her. "There's no comment because we know nothing. When there is something to tell, I'll give you the information. But for now, you need to move along."

The yellow lights of the tow truck from S&S Auto were seen well before the truck. There was a big wreath on the front of the truck grill and a small light up Christmas tree dangling from the rear-view mirror. The sharp reality that life and holidays still continued even in the depth of pain and sorrow hit my gut and I suddenly felt sick just thinking about what was going to take place in a few short minutes after the SUV was pulled from the river. Finn helped direct the driver after he'd talked to him about where the car was.

Edna Easterly didn't give two hoots about space or even what I'd said. She was snapping photos and asking the tow-truck driver all sorts of questions. Finn backed Edna away.

The big burly man with a curly mullet that I'd dealt with before got out of the tow truck after he drove down to where I was waiting for him. He wore a pair of blue mechanic overalls that were exactly what I'd seen him in before.

"Sheriff," He eyed me, not making the same mistake he'd done when he met me a year ago by brushing me off since I was a girl. "Looks like we got us an SUV to pull out."

"It appears that way." I wasn't one for small talk. I just wanted to get the car out of the river and get on with this investigation of the homicide.

"He's so country he thinks a seven-course meal is a possum and a six-pack." Poppa joked about the truck driver but I didn't laugh like I normally would. All eyes were on me and my every single move, facial movement and breath. "Kenni-Bug," Poppa noticed my solemn attitude. "Honey, this is going to be hard, but it's part of your job. You've got to spit-shine that star these citizens voted you in to wear and get a stiff upper lip. They need your strength. The strength you innately have in you."

I gulped, holding back the tears, and rubbed my finger over my five-point star. I drew on my inner guidance to get the energy and courage I needed when I heard the tow truck start to rev up to get a little closer to the edge of the water. I made sure my face was stern as I watched the man pull on a pair of waders and boots. He got into the water with big chains over his shoulder. He hooked them up to the hitch of Leighann's car.

When he got out, he took off the waders and boots and flipped the switch on the truck. The buzz of the chains clinking together made my heart beat faster and faster as they jerked up the end of Leighann's car up and out of the water. The water-logged SUV was dragged up to the ramp, spewing out water.

Sean Graves took a few steps forward, only to be greeted by the stiff arm of Scott. I couldn't help but notice Finn's face when Scott did something that normally Finn would do. There was a sense that Finn was glad he wasn't the one trying to stop Sean Graves.

"Let's take a look inside," I whispered to Finn and took the first step forward with him following behind me.

There was mud so thick that it covered the hood and the doors. I slipped on a pair of gloves and so did Finn. It was crucial to preserve anything we could. Though Finn didn't realize how crucial.

I ran my finger down along the creases of the driver's side door before I opened it.

"Empty." My brows furrowed.

"Thank, God," Finn's breath he'd been holding let out a long audible sigh.

The windows of the SUV were also covered in mud and though the sun had come out, it was still dark in the SUV. I unsnapped the flashlight from my holster and shined in the back. My heart fell to my feet when I saw Leighann in the very back. It was her beautiful red hair with the shimmery flecks of the silver tinsel that I'd noticed in her hair at the dance that told me it was her.

I pulled out of the SUV and handed Finn my flashlight.

"What is it, Kenni?" I heard Sean scream out my name from behind me. "Is she in there? God don't tell me she's in there!"

There was something about facing a father to tell him that his daughter was dead that didn't make me like my job.

When I turned around to look at him, it only took a split-second eye contact to take the man to his knees.

Chapter Six

"Do you promise you're going to find out what happened? How am I going to tell Jilly?" Sean ran his hands through his hair and wiped them over his mouth. Sean Graves begged and pleaded with me, "Promise me, Sheriff."

"I promise I'm going to try and figure out what happened." I knew it was going to be hard and any crime was a lot like a puzzle. There were pieces that fit here and there, it was trying to figure out where those pieces went that took the longest.

"I can't understand it. She was such a good driver." His nostrils rose and fell with each hard breath he took. "How am I going to tell Jilly?" His face crunched together, his lips rolled underneath his teeth, his jaw set and tears welled up in his eyes. He dragged the sleeve of his jacket across his eyes, blinking several times to keep the tears at bay.

It took about thirty minutes for Finn and Scott to clear the scene of the residents that'd come down to see what was going on. It took a whole lot longer to get Sean Graves to let Scott take him home. Took me even longer to gather my wits about me. Leighann Graves was the youngest homicide I'd ever had and I wanted to scream from the top of my lungs. Who on earth ended this young life too soon? Only, I knew I couldn't. I couldn't even tell my deputy that she was murdered.

We didn't touch the body until Max Bogus, the owner of the only funeral home in Cottonwood and our town's coroner, got there. There were steps that needed to be taken and I was going to make sure this one was by the books.

"How do you know some of these things?" Finn asked with a perplexed look.

"What things?" I asked back and tried not to get lost into his big brown eyes.

"You really thought she was in there, like you knew. You sure you're not one of them voodoo women?" He joked while we waited for Max to get Leighann's body on the church cart.

Max wore his typical khakis with a button-down shirt. This time he had on a V-neck sweater, probably due to the cold weather, and a heavy coat. His black rimmed glasses fogged with each breath he took.

"I guess it was just all the lack of contact Leighann had given over the past few hours." Lines creased in my forehead as my brows dipped. "It was like her to run off from her parents' house, but not like her to disappear completely."

I hated myself for lying to him. But I wasn't sure how he'd take it if I said that my Poppa, the ghost, told me. That's just something I wasn't sure even how to go about telling him. Nor did I want him to think I was nuts and dump me. Just not on my Christmas list this year.

Max motioned for us to come over. His round face was tense.

"Well?" I asked wondering what he saw.

"Nothing that's really apparent. I'm going to take her to the morgue to run some quick tests like drugs and alcohol to see if she was drunk driving or high, but on the outside, she's in perfect condition." He pinched his lips together.

"You don't think it's a homicide?" Finn asked.

"It's strange that she was in the back. Though she could've floated back there if she didn't have her seatbelt on, I'm guessing. But how did her keys get in her pocket?" He used the end of his pen to pick up a set of keys that were resting next to her hand on the gurney. "I checked the ignition and there were no keys in it. Plus, the SUV is in park."

I looked down at the ground so they couldn't see the relief on my face. The keys in her pocket and car in park was just more evidence it was a homicide and the less I had to prove what I'd been calling my hunch...which was Poppa.

"We are going to be busy this Christmas." Poppa did a jig. "Selfishly, I was afraid I wouldn't get to wish you a Merry Christmas, but now I can sing to you!" He was giddy with delight. "Oh, you better watch out." Poppa's mouth formed a dramatic "O." "You better not cry."

I walked a few steps to get away from him. I knew he was sad about Leighann. There just comes a time after you see so many homicides that you have initial emotions, then you realize it's part of the job and it's like your heart gets hard. Or maybe it was the way your body and mind coped with the idea of death. Poppa had told me many times that I'd get used to seeing dead bodies, and the feelings would change over time.

Right now, Poppa wasn't being insensitive, he was just living what he'd always told me. He loved Christmas and he always made sure it was special for me, his only grandchild. Right now wasn't the time to discuss it, though I was happy to see him too. Not under these circumstances. Unfortunately, these were the only circumstances under which we were able to see each other.

"That is odd." Finn shook his head and ran his hand down his head, resting it on the back of his neck. It appeared to him now that some foul play had happened. "And it looks like the right rear panel of the car is gone."

"By goodness," I gasped, "You're right."

We spent the next hour or so combing the area for that panel or anyplace that appeared the car had hit for the panel to be knocked off. We used the chains from the tow truck to drag the area where he'd pulled the car from the water, but there wasn't anything in there.

"This is really strange," I said to my Poppa when I got into the Wagoneer and he was sitting in the passenger seat. I drove up and down the road very slow, scouring each side of the road to see if there was any sort of object she could've hit or even if the panel was on the side of the road somewhere. Anything that looked like it could've been hit with the car. "What are you thinking?"

"I was thinking that she was coming down the road and maybe a deer or something crossed in front of her car. She slammed on the breaks, sending her into a tailspin." Poppa retold stories I'd heard all over Cottonwood as a kid where someone's car got destroyed by a deer.

"That could be a possibility if her keys weren't in her pocket and not in the ignition." When I checked out the back of the car, it wasn't wet, and it was too cold out for the back to have dried that quickly. "And how does that explain how the car got in park and in the river?"

The thought of it made chills crawl up my spine and down my arm, forcing me to grip the wheel as I turned back towards the boat dock where Finn continued to look into the woods for anything.

"That's how we know it was a homicide. And we both know that foul play is here." He gestured between us. "This means that me and you need to play our little game."

The little game he was referring to was the back and forth we loved to do when I was a little girl and now that I was sheriff. In fact, every time he did ghost himself, we'd play the game and it helped get more clues for me to look into.

I got out of the Jeep and slammed the door.

"You're right. I've got to go see the Graves again. Not to mention Manuel and his mother." I sighed.

"I hope you're going to take a look at Juanita Liberty since she wasn't fond of the girl," Poppa said with a troubled face.

"She sure didn't make any bones about it," I added. "Not that she was going to admit that she killed Leighann."

There was a history between the Graves's and the Liberty's where neither family were happy with their child dating the other. Both claimed they wanted better for their children. Many times over the past year when Leighann was underage, I was called out to the Graves's house or the Liberty house due to Sean Graves's claiming Manuel had been trespassing or they were fighting.

"When I've been to the Liberty house to talk to Manuel and Juanita was there, she made it clear that she was just as unhappy as Sean Graves with the two dating." I gnawed on the inside of my cheek and turned the Wagoneer around to head back to the crime scene. "She certainly didn't say she wanted the girl dead."

"She didn't say she didn't. She just made it apparent she didn't like her." Poppa frowned. "Not that Viv would kill anyone, but she's not happy with Finn for taking you away in a few days. Juanita is a Mama bear like Viv."

"She did say that she wanted better for Manuel than working at a tow company. He did have a future in a football career." I signed. "If Juanita got rid of Leighann, maybe Manuel would rethink his future."

"And gives her a motive to kill Leighann." Poppa's words made me get a queasy stomach.

"I'll have Finn bring her into the department. I don't want to question her at home," I said and watched Finn walking towards my Jeep as we pulled back into Chimney Rock. "She's a single mom with those other two young boys."

Manuel had two younger brothers. One was in high school and the other was much younger and I wanted to say he was in elementary school.

"Who are you talking to?" Finn glanced around the inside of my Jeep.

"I wasn't talking." I tried to play it off.

"There was condensation coming from your mouth as you spoke." His face grew serious, his jaw tensed.

"I guess I was just going over things in my head and didn't realize I was saying it out loud." I smiled to hide the crazy I was feeling by trying to keep him and Poppa's conversations separate.

"You're going to have to tell him sooner or later. I'd prefer sooner so he'll high-tail it out of here and leave you alone. You can't be a good sheriff and be all goo-goo-eyed over this northern." Poppa snarled, putting up his dukes like he was going to pop Finn in the nose. "Taking you away from your Mama during Christmas. What was he thinking?" Poppa spit. "He wasn't thinking, that's what happened. He wasn't thinking of you and your family like he should be if his intentions are true."

"I don't have time for this," I muttered under my breath.

"Time for what?" Finn's head jerked up.

"This...murder." I stomped to cover my slip up. I cozied up to Finn and gave him a kiss on the cheek. "We are getting ready to go to visit your family. Which I can't wait for." I gave him an extra little squeeze when I wrapped my arms around him. "The last thing we need is an investigation hanging over our head during Christmas."

"Then it means that we're going to be stuck side by side for the next few days to get it solved." He smiled, those perfect teeth appeared and sent my heart into fluttering overdrive.

Those were teeth you didn't get around here from the dentist. It was one of Finn's best qualities besides his perfect parted short brown hair.

"Not on my dime you won't, buck-o!" Poppa yelled in Finn's ear.

Finn blinked his eyes and pulled his finger up to his ear, the one Poppa yelled in, and gave it a vigorous shake.

"Dang." He jerked. "There's a loud ringing in my ear."

"I'm sure it'll go away soon." I gave Poppa the stink eye. "Probably stress," I said to Finn.

"Fine. But when you summon me, I might not come." He ghosted away, but I knew better. There wasn't anything Poppa loved more than a good case. This was the makings of a good one because there were some strange clues that needed to be answered, like where was her back-side panel?

"What are you thinking up there in that noggin?" Finn was catching on to the Southern slang.

"After we get done here, I'm going to have you go get Juanita Liberty and bring her down to the department." I looked up and caught an unexpected look on his face. "Yeah. When I went by there this morning, she didn't have anything nice to say about Leighann. Plus all the history between the two women. With Leighann gone, I think she'll be happy."

"Happy? That's a morbid thing to say." Finn's brows furrowed.

"She wants more for Manuel than Cottonwood." I looked at Scott when he walked up.

"Didn't he have a big future in football?" Scott asked.

"He did and that's what Juanita is upset about. He didn't take the scholarship for college and she's upset about it." I looked up and noticed the clouds were taking on a gray color.

"Don't step on a mama's toes." Finn shrugged.

"A Southern mama's toes at that." Scott nodded. "They will go through hell or high water to see to it that their baby gets their due."

"Mmhmmmm," I ho-hummed in agreement.

Finn's gaze arched slowly back and forth between me and Scott like he was trying to decipher the conversation between us.

"It's Southern talk," I noted. "Finn's from Chicago."

"Oh." Scott's mouth formed an O, his chin lifted up. "We were sayin' that his Mama would do anything to..."

"Yeah. I get it." Finn glowered and turned away.

Scott and I stood there in silence as we watched Finn walk back down to where they'd pulled the SUV out of the water. He used the bottom of his boot to brush on top of the grass and his flashlight to focus on the ground as if he were looking for more clues or evidence.

"What's up with him?" Scott asked.

"He's a very good deputy. Very by the book." I noted and tried not to get the vibe that Finn wasn't too interested in Scott or his help. "If you don't mind, why don't you head back to the department and get the paperwork started for the case. Let's treat it like a homicide until Max tells us otherwise."

"No problem." Scott glanced at Finn before he gave me the nod and headed out.

"What was that about?" I asked Finn when I walked down to talk to him.

"It's weird seeing another person on the team. Not that we couldn't use it right now, but I felt like an outsider." Finn smiled. "Stupid really."

"I'm sorry I made you feel that way. I never intended it." Softly, I touched his arm. "I think it's super cute that you still try to figure out what we're saying."

"I think it's more of my jealousy that you communicate with him in a different language or something." Finn smiled. "That's all."

"I'll communicate with him in any way as long as we can get this murder solved before we leave for Chicago." I turned it around to a positive, so any sort of negative feelings Finn was having wouldn't hurt the momentum of the investigation.

"Where do we start?" Finn rubbed his hands together.

"We need to find that side panel, we need to figure out who Leighann and Manuel were fighting with last night and we need to know what they were fighting about." Everything I was saying was just the basics that'd help put any sort of pieces together.

"You don't think the panel is somewhere in the water?" He asked a really good question.

"I don't because the back of the SUV isn't wet. It appears the front end went in, stuck in the mud and sort of drifted a few feet from the put in. I don't think the side panel fell off when it went into the water. What did it hit to make it fall off?" So many questions were stabbing me.

Solving a murder was like a giant puzzle. It was up to me

and the deputies to put those pieces together. Unfortunately, the pieces didn't always fit together in a nice little way and hopefully Leighann's body and a few answered questions were going to get it completed.

"Juanita is your first thought?" Finn asked.

"She'd be the one with the highest priority of motive since Leighann is the one who had the most influence on Manuel and his life. The Graves told me this morning that they'd accepted the relationship," I noted.

"You believe them even after the look on their faces from the dance last night?" Finn folded and crossed his arms across his chest.

"They'd given Leighann a job and Manuel still had his job, so I do believe they've accepted it. Not that it means they still didn't want better for Leighann, but to kill their own daughter?" I questioned. I just couldn't go there at this time. I inhaled deeply, "I don't think they were so mad to kill their own flesh and blood."

"I agree with you, but what happened to no stone unturned?" His features hardened as he threw my own mantra back at me.

"That's why we are going to question everyone. Including the Graves again." My eyebrows dipped in a frown. "While you go get Juanita, I think I'll stop by the Graves's. Check on them and maybe ask a few questions now that it's turned from finding her to finding out what happened to her. I'm sure the entire Auxiliary Women's club is there with food and people stopping by."

When someone died in Cottonwood, the entire town rallied around each other. Immediately, the Auxiliary Women's club would get to work in the kitchen, taking many dishes to the family.

"I'll give you about an hour and continue to just comb the area while you do that. I'll pick up Juanita on my way back." His gaze softened.

After we said our goodbyes, I got into the Wagoneer and headed back to the Graves's house.

Their driveway was already filled with cars from Cottonwood citizens there to give their condolences. This was when it was really great to be from a small town. There might've been a lot of gossip, but whenever there was a tragedy, we put our differences aside and pulled together to help the family and community get through it. Though Leighann was an adult, she was still just a child and there was something wrong about the death of a child before the parents.

Instead of knocking, I just let myself in. The family room was filled. Mayor Chance Ryland and his new bride, Polly, were sitting in chairs that were in front of the couch, talking to Jilly and Sean. No doubt they were telling them that the department, me, was going to do everything in our power to get to the bottom of what happened.

I headed back to the kitchen to find Viola White, Ruby Smith, and Mama logging all the food that was being delivered to the house. They would write down who brought what food and would label the dish they'd brought it in. This whole food repass thing was also sort of a competition between the women on who got the most compliments. I knew it was a messed-up theory, but that's how the pride of these Southern women worked.

"The broccoli salad is from Bev Tisdale." Mama lifted the lid and her nose turned up. "We can just throw that one away. I can smell the store-bought ingredients."

"Sounds good to me." Viola grabbed the tin and tossed it in the black garbage bag in her other hand. "What about what Polly brought?"

Mama lifted the foil off the plate that Polly must've brought as a good gesture.

"Ugh. I can't even make it out." Mama didn't bother putting the tin foil back on it. "Pitch it. What's wrong with people?"

I could spot Mama's famous chicken pot pie from anywhere. And she sure did love to boast about it since it was now on the menu at Ben's Diner and featured on the Culinary Channel. I was proud of her too. But the other women were green with envy.

"Kenni," Mama's voice rose when she saw me. She rushed over with her hands out in front of her. Viola and Ruby rushed over too, their ears on full alert. "Everyone wanted me to call you and ask you what happened, but I knew you'd be busy."

"Tell us." Viola held out a piece of her homemade potato candy that she knew I couldn't resist. It was a Southern classic favorite and her homemade peanut butter was to die for. "Here." She stuck the napkin in my hand.

"There's not much to tell." I took a bite of the candy and was thankful when Myrna Savage came into the kitchen with an armful of flowers.

"Help me," she squealed when she noticed the women were standing there looking at me. "I've got a van full of flowers."

Myrna Savage was the owner of Petal Pushers, the only florist in town.

I grabbed one of the vases out of her hand and stuck it on the window sill next to a prescription bottle of Ambien that belonged to Sean. Poor guy probably had a hard time sleeping, I waved my concern for him away.

"Come on, Viv." Myrna grabbed Mama by the sleeve. "I need your help."

Mama would normally protest but under the circumstances, she bit her lip and hurried out the door beside Viola and Ruby.

"Honey, how are you?" Myrna asked and pulled a piece of baby's breath out of her black hair.

"I'm alright. It's a shame to see a young person come to their demise before they should," I said and glanced over her shoulder at the medication bottle on the kitchen window sill.

"Honey, I wholeheartedly believe that when it's your time, it's your time." She nodded her head and in her own way, I knew she was trying to come to grips with it herself. "Jilly is a strong woman. I'm not so sure that Sean's interior is as tough as his exterior, but he's gonna need a lot of help. I done told Dr. Shively that she's gonna have to give him something." She continued to nod, "if you know what I mean."

"My goodness," Mama fanned her hand in front of her face when she walked into the kitchen with a couple flower arrangements. "I used to love flowers, but now the smell reminds me of a funeral home."

I didn't let the women continue to fuss and argue over where to put the flowers. I took it upon myself to take them from Mama and put them on the window sill right next to the prescription bottle. Upon further inspection of the label, it appeared Sean Graves's prescription was written by Dr. Camille Shively.

I headed back into the family room. The room was filled with low murmurs and everyone seemed to be facing the Graves, who were sitting on the couch with Mayor Ryland and Polly next to them. In the chairs next to fireplace was Angela Durst, the secretary for Graves's Towing. Her daughter, Beka, was in the chair next to her. Both of them looked up at me with turned down mouths. Angela blinked a couple of knowing blinks. There were a few Baptist nods from other people who were there to give their condolences.

"Mayor, Polly." I greeted them and set any difference the three of us had aside. It wasn't a secret that we butted heads a few times over the course of my terms. "Sean, Jilly, can I talk to you?"

I saw Polly shift in her chair and straighten up as though she were getting herself ready to hear something.

"In private?" I asked.

"Of course." Jilly jumped up and tugged on Sean's shirt. "We can go into the office."

The office was in the other side of the old house and I'd been in there a few times. Including the time I'd caught Leighann and Manuel in there being a little more intimate than her parents probably wanted her to be. Actually, not probably, I knew for certain they didn't want Leighann near Manuel.

From the photos of Leighann and Manuel that were framed in the office that weren't there before, it sure looked like those times had changed.

After they shut the office door to give us some privacy, Sean started in with the questions.

"What happened? There had to be foul play." He insisted. Jilly did her best to calm him down, but he kept saying that she'd never take her own life.

"She did say she was going to a few times," Jilly's voice cracked.

Was it possible that Poppa was here during a situation where they did take their own lives? It's something we'd never come across and he certainly wasn't around right now to hear this.

"That's enough, Jilly." Sean's jaw tensed, and he glared at his wife. "Our daughter didn't do this to herself."

"There's not much I can tell you about any preliminary reports from Max," I referred to the coroner, "But I can tell you that her car keys were in her pocket, the shift was in park and there were no visible signs of a homicide."

"You." Jilly jumped up and shook a finger at Sean. Her face was lit on fire. "You did this to our daughter. She told you that you were the one who'd make her take her life and now she has."

"Jilly, Sean." I had to calm them down. "A death is very hard. I'm sure the death of a child is something that is unfathomable. But right now, I need you two to help me figure out exactly what happened. And being at each other's throats isn't going to get us anywhere."

Jilly sat back down and planted her hands between her knees.

"Kenni is right." Sean did the right thing by going over to his wife, bending down and taking her into his arms.

"We don't know if there's foul play or not. But we do know that it's awfully strange for her to drive off the boat ramp, put her car in park and put her keys in her pocket." I wanted to try and give them some information that would trigger anything. "When we did a little more investigation on the car after it was pulled out, we noticed the right back panel was missing."

By the look on Sean's face, I could tell he didn't know.

"Did Leighann have an accident that day?" I asked.

"No." Sean shook his head. "In fact, she was washing her car because she'd said that she saw on the weather channel a snow storm coming. She put a sealer on it to keep off the snow and the salt that would get on her car while it was bad out."

"Did she act funny? Or talk to anybody that day? Anybody?" I asked.

"Rachel Palmer came by, but she always comes over." Jilly shrugged and wiped her eyes with her hands.

"She did before she went off to college. It's not like they've been great friends since they graduated." Sean corrected his wife.

"Did you hear anything they were saying?" I asked and wrote down Rachel's name. I knew her parents from church. Nice people.

"I watched from the office window out there, but then we got a call about a tow and I went ahead and dispatched it out to Manuel because I really think it's important," Jilly swallowed hard, "was important that Leighann kept in touch with her friends outside of Manuel."

"I see that y'all seem to have accepted Manuel and Leighann's relationship." I picked up one of the frames off the credenza.

"This was where Leighann worked on paperwork and we let her make it her own." Jilly's lips turned into a little smile. "She was excited to have her own space. I even took her to the Dollar Shop in Clay's Ferry to get her frames for cheap. The first thing she did was go down to Dixon's Foodtown and use their photo machine where you can hook up your cell phone and get the pictures right off of it."

"It wasn't that we didn't want her to date him. But like Jilly said, we felt like she was losing her friends. She spent so much time with him and she had a scholarship to go to the community college, but she didn't want to do that." There was disappointment on his face. "Maybe if we made her go, we wouldn't be here right now."

"Some kids don't go to college now, Sean." Jilly sucked in a deep breath. The frustration was visible. Her lips tightened. "We told her she didn't have to. Maybe next year. We thought that once she saw how hard it was to have a full-time job, she'd rethink the whole college thing."

"What do you know about Manuel's college?" I asked.

"You know he was such a good football player. It's true. They met here. He's a good worker. But when I saw him and Leighann kissing a couple years ago, I lost it. I made sure he was busy when Leighann was here. I gave her extra money, so she didn't have to come to work. I tried so hard to keep them apart," Sean said.

"They were just kids." Jilly tried to soften Sean's words for him. This was something she'd often do in public. "We thought it would end."

"We thought wrong. After a few months of that is when Leighann started acting up and sneaking off. She was saying how much she loved him, and no one was going to keep them apart. I didn't know who he was coming in here and messing up our lives that we had planned out." Sean appeared to be as mad today as he was the first time I'd gotten a call from him about putting the boy in jail.

"I've reminded Sean how many times that we were no different." There Jilly went again making him look better.

"Times were different then, Jillian." That's the first time I'd ever heard him call her by her full name. "Prices were cheaper. We got this from my family. Leighann was throwing her life away on a boy."

Jilly buried her head in her hands. "She'll never know what it's like to hold her own baby. We will never be grandparents," she screamed towards Sean. "I swear if she took her own life...but you said she was in the back." She looked at her husband. He nodded. "She always wore her seatbelt. There was never a time she didn't. It's me that forgets, and she wouldn't even start the car until everyone had a seatbelt on."

"This doesn't appear to be getting you anywhere," Poppa ghosted himself next to the desk. "What was the relationship between Sean and Leighann like recently?"

"What was your relationship with Leighann over the past six months since she didn't go off to college?" I asked.

"I told her that if she didn't go to college that she was going to pay for her own cell phone, get on the company's payroll, pay her own insurance on that SUV and health." He appeared to have realized how bad that sounded because he looked down.

"And she had to pay rent." Jilly looked up at me. "He told her that she had to pay rent on her own bedroom."

"I was trying to scare her into going to college. It's no different than what the experts tell you to do." He ran his hand through his hair.

"Did she have the money to do those things?" I asked.

"She worked all the time. She'd do dispatch at night, but if it was a call that was an emergency, like a car wreck that needed us, either me or Manuel would come out," Sean said.

"Tell her." Jilly growled. "Tell her how you packed up Leighann's clothes and told her to move in with Manuel until she paid her rent."

"Is that true?" I was beginning to see a side of Sean Graves that I didn't think he wanted me to see. A side that maybe said he and his daughter weren't on the best terms.

"I'm ashamed now, but yes. She and Manuel lived out of the SUV for a while. I guess they were taking spit baths in the employee sink or something because I'd gotten a phone call from Juanita," He referred to Manual's mother, "and she told me that she wasn't letting my daughter live in that house because she ruined her son's life."

"That's when Sean told her that her son ruined our daughter's life and squashed her dreams. It was a mess." Jilly's brows furrowed, the crease between them deepened. "Juanita's other son came over here with a gun and knives strapped to him saying that Sean better not disrespect their Mama again."

I made sure I'd gotten everything they were saying on the notepad. It was enough evidence, if true, to think that one of the Liberty's had done something to Leighann. They were big boys and very protective of family. Though I couldn't rule out Sean. "Did you ever hit your daughter?" I asked. Before he could protest, because he was revving up, I followed up by saying, "I understand how heated things can get as a teen. I've been there with my parents. If you did do something, I understand, but I'm gonna need you to tell me now. Not in a few days from now when I've spent all this time looking for someone who killed her. If you did hurt your daughter, I know you didn't mean to, but..."

"You hold it right there, Sheriff." He pointed his finger at me and took a step forward.

"Whoa, diggity-dog," Poppa ghosted between us. "You move one more step towards my Kenni-Bug and I'll put a haunting on you that would scare them zombies in that tv show."

"Please remove your finger from my face," I said in a stern and steady voice.

He dropped his hand.

"If you think I hurt Leighann in anyway physically, you are wrong. I'll take a lie detector test right here, right now." His eyes didn't move. "I might've disapproved of her boyfriend, but I'd never hurt her."

"Have you ever laid a hand on Leighann?" I asked because he truly didn't answer the question. His dancing around it would suffice some, but not me.

"Sean," Jilly stood back up and placed her hand on her husband's back. "He can get a little upset at times."

His shoulders started to jump up and down. His chin fell to his chest. Her words were ringing true with him.

"At times he could get a little out of control. He can break things and he can yell really loud. He's even back handed me and Leighann a time or two." She rubbed his back vigorously. "But he is a good, hardworking man. He's been a wonderful provider. He makes sure we have everything we want. He puts food on the table and we've never been in debt. I'm confident that he didn't hurt our daughter."

"Your daughter is dead," I reminded her. She might've been making herself and Sean feel good with her excuses of why he was such a jack-donkey, but I just couldn't let it go.

"You nasty sonofa..." Poppa's words strung together. He could never stand for a man hitting a woman.

"This is the time to come clean with anything you need to tell me, because her body will reveal the answers. If her body tells me that someone hurt her, you're the first person I'm going to come after." It wasn't a threat, it was the gods to honest truth. "I saw you and Jilly at the dance last night. I saw the two of you get up and walk out without saying good bye to Leighann and you looked upset."

"I didn't hurt Leighann." His chin drew back up and he locked eyes with me. "Like I said, I'm more than happy to go down to the department and take a lie detector test."

Chapter Seven

"He's the only hell his Mama raised." Poppa was spittin' mad when we got back into the Jeep. "Sean Graves is a tricky man."

I'd left out the office door and walked around to my Jeep because I was so thrown back by how volatile Sean's relationship was with the women in his life that I just couldn't force myself to make small talk with the town folk there to support him without me saying something about his true character.

"I'm guessing you know something about him?" I asked.

It was kinda good that Poppa was the sheriff before me because he knew the parents and grandparents of people my age.

"You know how he bugs you about Leighann and Manuel? Well, Jilly's parents did same thing about him. When I was in your shoes, they told me he hit her, but she'd never fess up to it when I'd go to her house and question her." He drummed his fingers along the window sill of the passenger side door. "She had some sort of home economics scholarship to a higher learning school and if I remember correctly, she didn't go because of Sean. Her grandfather didn't go to the wedding. It was small. I remember I was down at the Moose having a drink when he came in. He put down the awfulest sight of clear you ever saw." Poppa shook his head in disgust. "He said how much he wanted more for his granddaughter than the old Graves family."

"What did he mean?" I asked.

"Honey, them Graves are as rough as the Libertys." His eyes lowered, and he slowly turned his head to look out the window. "It sure is gonna look so pretty around here when that snow comes."

He changed the subject to yet another subject I didn't want to discuss.

"There's not going to be any snow," I informed him. "Because you are going to go up there and plead with the big guy."

"Kenni-Bug, that's up to Mother Nature and trust me when I say that she's one stubborn brood." He threw his head back and laughed.

"Snow or not, killer caught or not, I'm going to Chicago with Finn." I flipped the turn signal on right and turned south on Main Street. "We need to get back to the department. Finn is bringing in Juanita Liberty. We can ask her about them boys of hers going to the Graves with their weapons. You let me do that talking and you just ghost yourself on over into a corner," I warned Poppa when I parked the car in the alley behind the department.

Juanita and Betty were talking about some sort of recipe when I walked in. Juanita's face stared me down as I made my way over to them.

"Go on," Juanita didn't even let me get my coat off before she started to hound me. "Ask me what you want. I've got stuff to do tonight."

"Juanita," I looked her square in the face.

"Kenni-Bug," Poppa whispered in my ear. "Breathe in Jesus, breathe out peace." It was his way of telling me not to lose my cool.

I adjusted my thoughts and took the tape recorder out of the top drawer of my desk. I pushed record and sat it on the edge of the desk closest to Juanita. There wasn't a word I wanted to miss.

"Juanita." I planted my hands on the desk and leaned over her way as she sat in the chair. "I've got a dead girl on my hands. It appears to be awfully suspicious. It happens to be about a young woman you didn't care for. I've got a few questions for you and it might take me a few minutes or up to hours. It all depends on how much you cooperate."

"If you're wondering if I've got an alibi or hurt Leighann Graves in anyway, I didn't and I do have an alibi. I was with my boys last night at the dance and then at home." She looked at her watch. "Which is where I need to be right now. You can ask any of my boys."

I slid my gaze over her shoulder at Scott. He was writing something down, which I assumed was some of her statement.

"About those boys." I decided not to press her too much on where she was and who she was with last night until I got the particulars about the autopsy from Max Bogus. "Tell me about the time they showed up at the Graves's house with guns," I told her.

Sometimes it was best not to give the whole hand, but to give just enough of a push or poke in hopes it would prompt her to do something that'd lead me to a clue or lead in the case. Besides, I wasn't so sure she had anything to do with Leighann's death.

She eased back in the chair as her head slowly tilted to the other side of her shoulders. Her mouth slightly opened, and I could see her tongue fiddling with her back teeth.

"Sean Graves had said some not so nice things about their mama." She slid her body up to the edge of the chair, leaned in towards me, and stared me square in the eyes. "When you heard people talking about your mama's recent situation, didn't that burn you up?" She asked. "Didn't that make you want to draw your pistol on them to shut their mouths? Just because my boys took up for me, doesn't mean I killed no one. Just like your Mama didn't kill no one."

"Did I say you killed someone?" I asked.

"You didn't have to. Don't mistake my accent or my living arrangements for stupidity. I'm far from ignorant and I know what's going on here." She looked around. "My son's girlfriend is dead. Apparently murdered, or you wouldn't be here snooping around. Me and Leighann didn't get along. She kept my boy from making it big in life and for what? A tow company?" Her shoulders jerked as she let out a chuckle. "Honestly, I don't know what he likes about working there. I've been on some late-night runs with him when he had to take the overnight shift and got paid minimum wage. I swear. He should've taken that scholarship. His future would've been so much better. But, just because that's my opinion and I didn't like how she has a hold on my boy, doesn't mean I wanted her dead."

"Did you hear that?" Poppa ghosted next to me. "She said has a hold on my boy. Present tense. She didn't do it."

One little hint we learned in the academy was not only to watch people's body language when you were interrogating them but to listen carefully to their words.

"If it's all the same to you, I'd like to talk to your children.

What is a good time to come out to your house?" I asked and ignored Poppa who was now pacing in front of the desk between me and Juanita.

"We've got barely little time since the tree lot is going full blast for the high school football team. You're more than welcome to come by there. Plus, we could use an extra set of hands. I'll let you talk to Jonathon because he's old enough to know what's going on, but my little one is off limits. He's too young to even understand what's going on." She put her hands on her knees and pushed up to stand. "Will that be all?"

"Thank you for coming in." I didn't bother getting up. I just leaned back in my chair and stared at the blank white board.

"Oh dear," Betty groaned. "Remember last year's tree lot?"

"What happened last year?" There was a bit of a worried tone to Finn's question.

"Yeah?" Scott followed up.

"Go on, Kenni, you tell them." Betty's brows rose.

"I think you're better than me at telling it." I shrugged and got up to walk over to the white board.

"Well, last year we got a call from Sean Graves about Leighann and Manuel. It was an all-out brawl." As Betty told the story, I wrote Leighann Graves name in the middle of white board.

Just like we'd been doing since Finn insisted on us using one, I made a big circle around her name and drew out line extensions from it.

On one I wrote Juanita Liberty, another I wrote Manuel Liberty, another I wrote Sean Graves and the last one I wrote girl at the party, who we'd yet to identify.

"Manuel was playing Santa for the little children and Leighann was in an elf suit." Betty rolled her eyes and shook her head at the same time. "Sean had gone to drag Leighann home, like some daddy caveman, but not without him and Manuel getting into a fuss. All sorts of kids were crying. Sean'd pulled Manuel's Santa beard off. It was a mess. Trees were falling over, and the strung lights had been jerked down from them fussin' and fightin'. It was like one of them crazy reality television shows where all them women catfight and all."

"What is your reasoning for putting Sean up there?" Scott asked.

"According to him and Jilly, the relationship with Sean and Leighann hasn't been any less than rocky and volatile at times. Maybe she and Sean got into an argument, nothing new, but this time it was the straw that broke the camel's back."

"Don't you know," Betty looked over at Scott and eased herself up out of her chair. "What's always done in the dark always finds its way to the light. That's what my mama, and her mama, and her mama used to say."

"It rings true every time." Poppa nodded and agreed right along with Betty. "Now put on there about Manuel looking at the phone and all."

"Oh, good one," I said and totally forgotten Manuel had said that.

"Good one?" Finn eyeballed me.

"I just remembered something, and I was saying it to myself." I sucked in a deep breath and got composure before I wrote down what Poppa had reminded me about. "When I was visiting with Manuel. He said that he'd gone through Leighann's phone before he gave it to the Graves. There could've been something on there erased. I think we need to get a subpoena to the cell phone service to retrieve any information we can."

"I can do that. I've had plenty of work with those things at the reserve," Scott spoke up and started to write down something in his notebook.

"Betty," I stopped Betty, who was preparing to go for the night. "Did you set Scott up on the database with a password so he can just go into the file and pull up Leighann's case?"

"I sure did," she said and pulled on her coat. "You good?" She asked Scott.

While they finalized some things, Duke woke up from his nap after he heard his name and stretched out on his dog bed.

When he noticed it was me, he pushed his paws forward and stuck his butt up in the air, doing a real downward dog position like those crazy pretzel ladies in those yoga classes do. His mouth gaped open into a big yawn before he got up on all fours and trotted over to me.

"Any news from Max?" I asked Betty and took a treat from the treat jar that Finn had on his desk for Duke. I flipped him a treat and gave him a good scrub on the head.

"Are you kidding me? You'd be the first after me to hear," she tsked. "I'm giving you fair warning, this is all the talk around town and when you get to the church, I'm sure you'll get asked a lot of questions."

"I think I can handle them." I was pretty confident I could, but I still appreciated Betty's concern, even though I knew there was a deeper meaning behind it.

"Are you sure you don't want to tell me anything, so I can help keep the buzzards back?" She gave it another good old college try.

"I'm positive. Thank you for your quick work today. I truly appreciate it." It was my way of kicking her out without telling her to get out.

"Alrighty then. If you don't need me." She pushed her

pocketbook in the bend of her elbow and bent her arm up. "I've called Clay's Ferry Dispatch to take over."

"Thanks, Betty. I'll see you soon." I walked over and held the door open for her. "Stay," I instructed Duke when he stuck his nose out of the door to get a smell of the fresh air.

"Before I go." She put her hand on the door to stop it from shutting. "I'm heading on down to Dixon's. I had Toots Buford hold me back some bread. Do you want me to pick you up something before the big storm?"

"Nope." My lips parted to say something else, but I slammed by mouth shut, followed by the shutting door. "If I hear one more person say they believe this storm of the century is really coming, I'm might go into a tizzy."

"It's supposed," Scott started to say.

"Aaaa," I wiggled my finger. "Don't speak it out into the world."

"What are you talking about?" Finn asked and walked over to the white board. He picked up the blue marker and took the top off.

"You know all that new age mumbo-jumbo about think positive thoughts and it'll come true." I watched both of them nod at me but not without looking as if they thought I'd lost my mind. "Anyways, I'm positive the storm is going to scoot down a skoosh and hit Tennessee really hard or move up a smidgen and hit Ohio, bypassing all of Kentucky."

"It clearly looks like..." Scott started again before I put my palm flat out in front of him.

"Not another word about the weather while you are in my department because we've got to focus on solving what happened to Leighann Graves." I sucked in air to fill my lungs and slowly let it out. A relaxation tip that Tina Bowers had given me a few months ago when she said I needed to get rid of stress.

"Then let's get started." Finn and Scott gave each other a strange look but I chose to ignore it because it wasn't worth getting into. "What's your thoughts?"

"My thoughts are that she was placed in her car after she'd passed out or died. Something. Her Mama insists that she always wore her seat belt." I talked as Finn wrote under Leighann's name. Duke realized we weren't leaving and he got back in his bed for another nap. "The keys were in her pocket."

"Did she have a reason to end her life?" Scott asked.

"That's what I was saying before." I hated for this motive to leave my mouth, but I couldn't help but remember that in the academy they always said that more times than not, people were murdered by the hands of a loved one. "Leighann had a very rocky relationship with her dad."

He moved his hand over to the motives section under Sean's name.

"Jilly confessed that Sean did use some physical attempts to get his point across." I didn't want to say it. It was so hard for me to wrap my brain around.

"He was an abuser." Scott did a much better job getting it out. "Jerk."

I proceeded to read off my notes, so my words wouldn't be biased. The internal feeling I was feeling for Sean Graves was not kind. I wanted to make sure this investigation went by the book and me not be accused of harboring hard feelings towards him.

"You mean to tell me that he admitted to striking his daughter?" Finn asked. "I'd never thought it."

"Me either, but I could tell something was off. I mean all those times we went there. Manuel once said to me that he had to get her out of the house. That stuck with me. I wonder if that's what he was talking about." I had to see Manuel again.

I would question him when I went back out to question Juanita.

"I want you to put Manuel's brother on the list too. Jonathon did pull that gun on Sean." I didn't like hearing how he'd used a gun to get a point across and I'd make sure he had gun permits.

Most of the residents of Cottonwood packed heat. That wasn't an issue at all, it was the ones that didn't have the right permits that bothered me most.

I wrapped up the information I'd gotten from the Sean and Jilly and that included the confrontation with the Graves.

"This is like modern day Hatfield and McCoys." Scott rubbed his hands together. "Dude, why didn't you tell me this was the good stuff instead of how we sit around the reserve."

"You never asked," Finn replied.

It never dawned on me that the two of them knew each other until this exact moment.

"You two know each other. Huh." I felt my jaw drop and my eyes lower before I quickly brought them back to their normal position.

"We would pass each other in the halls but never worked a case until now." Scott was a lot more excited than Finn.

"Glad you are here. We expect you'll be just fine while we are gone." I turned back to Finn and smiled. This had been a long time coming and I couldn't wait to meet his family.

"We ready to go?" Scott jumped to his feet.

"Whoa, buddy." Finn put the top back on the marker. "It doesn't work that way around here."

"Right. First, we have to get the report back from Max that

proves Leighann's murder is a homicide. If the report comes back, which I expect that it will, then we go and start asking questions." It was the small-town way of policing. It took Finn a lot of months to figure that out when he was hired to be my deputy. I too believed in my gut and followed my instinct, but since my Poppa was here, I really trusted my gut.

"On my rounds in the morning, I'll go back the funeral home and see if Max has anything unless he calls first." Sometimes he did call first, but I'd yet to hear from him. "Depending on if he has any new information will determine my day and who I see. For now, I've got to get to the church and Finn's got to get Duke home."

"What do I need to do?" Scott asked.

"I'm guessing you can go on back to the hotel." I knew we'd put him up at the Tattered Book and Inn down the street. "Or you can go help us set up."

"I think I'll grab a to-go dinner from Bartleby and go get some sleep." He pushed himself up to standing. "I'll be here in the morning."

"Thanks for all your help today. You got thrown into the fire and I really appreciate you taking care of Sean." It was hard for me to even think we were so nice to him now, but I stood by the innocent until proven guilty.

He was guilty of that since he admitted to it and that didn't make me happy.

"No problem. I kinda wish I wasn't so nice now." He only said what we were all thinking.

While he got his stuff together, Finn and I both cleaned up our desks and did a few here and there chores to tidy up the place to get ready for tomorrow.

"Do you really think Sean did it?" Finn asked as soon as

Scott closed the door between the department and the restaurant.

I walked over and locked the door.

"I think the families had a feud between them and given time, I'm not so sure Leighann and Manuel would've stuck it out." I walked up to him and put my arms around him.

"Do you think she was tired of being in the middle? She was tired of trying to figure out where she was going to rest her head next?" He looked down at me. "She put the SUV in neutral. Once the car was somewhat submerged in the front, she put the car in park and took out the keys." He acted out the movie playing in his head. "Then she climbed in the back of the SUV in a little bit of a panic because she realized what she was doing wasn't right and climbed to get out and stuck the keys in her pocket, it was the point of no return and she drowned."

"You big dummy." Poppa appeared. "No. That's not what happened." He put his hands under each armpit and started to walk around like a chicken, flapping his elbows in and out. "He's lost his mind. We hear you cluckin' boy, but we can't find your nest."

Poppa walked around Finn and me in circles, clucking and doing his chicken dance. My nose started to flare like it did when I tried not to laugh out loud. My lips pinched in between my teeth, but I let go on his last cluck and busted out laughing, taking a step backwards.

"Kenni, honey?" Finn cautiously asked. "Are you okay?"

"Don't you honey, my Kenni-Bug." Poppa's clucking and chicken dance had stopped, and I got my composure together.

"Finley Vincent." I forced myself not to laugh. "It'll be our luck if this darn weather system does dump on us." I turned it around to make him think I was laughing like a crazy person.

"Now you've got that stinkin' thinkin'." Finn used my own phrase on me. "Where's my little optimistic girlfriend?"

"I guess I've heard everyone that I've encountered today say something about this snow and it's starting to sink in my soul." Now I was back to thinking about that dumb weather forecast.

"We will be able to drive to the airport and get on that big bird that'll take us all the way to Midway Airport." He was good at trying to reassure me. "They won't ground the planes."

"You are my hero." I curled up on my toes and took his promise with a sealed kiss.

My phone chirped from my back pocket and I grabbed it. It was a text from Max Bogus.

"It's Max." I showed my phone to Finn. "He's got a preliminary report ready."

"Let's go." Finn read my mind. He patted his leg. "Let's go, Duke."

Chapter Eight

"Is Max working late?" Finn asked when we turned down Main Street towards the one-stop shop funeral home.

"I recon." As sad as it was, death still came without being murdered and from what I'd heard last night, the grim reaper had come to take a few of our elder citizens during the holiday. "Seems that he's all full up with funerals, so he must be doing the autopsy when he has moments throughout his day."

Finn stared out the window. He had his left hand planted over Duke's body. My goofy dog had positioned himself between the front and back seat of the Jeep.

Finn put his hand on my shoulder. "You're going to love my family. They are already going to love you. My sister has told them all about you."

"I'm excited too." I sucked in a deep breath and tried to ignore that I suddenly realized I wasn't going to be home for the tree lighting. My stomach started to hurt.

"Feeling sick?" Poppa appeared in the back seat of the Jeep. Duke squirmed his way back next to poppa. He wagged his tail with glee. "Home sick?"

My eyes slid to the rear-view mirror and I stared at my Poppa. His eyes were soft. He always knew when I wasn't feeling well, even emotionally.

"What's wrong, boy?" Finn turned around in the seat and snapped his fingers for Duke to come so he could pat him. When he continued to bounce on Poppa's lap, Finn looked all sorts of confused. "Is he feeling okay?"

"He's fine. I swear he does weird stuff like that all the time in here and at the house." I watched in the rear-view mirror as Poppa pat on and scrubbed up under Duke's chest, sending the dog into a full-on howl. "Maybe he sees my Poppa's ghost or something."

Poppa's head jerked up and he looked at me in anticipation that I was going to tell Finn our little secret.

"I've heard dogs and kids can see things we can't. I'm not sure I can get behind that concept or not." Finn shrugged it off, letting me know that he wasn't quite ready for my secret life. I swallowed the lump in my throat, wondering if he'd ever be ready.

Poppa's shoulders slumped, and I peeled my eyes away from the mirror.

"I believe in spirits." It was a topic we'd never brought up. "I think..."

"Alright. Seriously? Right before we go into a funeral home full of dead bodies. I'm getting the heebie-jeebies just thinking about it." Finn grabbed his thermal mug out of the bean bag coffee holder and flipped the lid to take a drink. "You bringing this up now is just going to make me more on edge."

He reached up and turned the knob on the radio to make it a little louder.

"Good morning, Cottonwood. DJ Nelly coming at you this morning with some sweet sounds of this time of the year. The hustle and bustle can bring out the worst in us, so be sure to be kind. After all, Christmas is only a few days away and it looks like it's gonna be white." DJ Nelly had to've planned playing "White Christmas".

I hit the off button on the radio.

"You don't love 'White Christmas'?" Finn looked at me. "You sure are getting cranky. Are you sure you want to go to Chicago? Because you don't have to."

"No. I'm fine." I shook my head. "It's just that I don't want to jinx our trip and all this talk of snow and all the memories of how much fun a white Christmas around really is," I shook it off. "It's all just getting to me. That's all."

I put the shift into park after I pulled up behind Max's hearse.

"Kenni," Finn put his hand on my leg. "Really, honey. If you want to stay here, we can."

I bit the inside of my jaw so I wouldn't say anything.

"I know you want to go to Chicago. But I also know you love tradition. I truly think it's born and bred in you Southern women." His gaze softened and he smiled, making my insides explode with how lucky I was to have him in my life.

"Puh-leeeeeese," Poppa's sarcasm dripped. "I used that old song and dance on your granny."

"You were saying?" I asked and ignored Poppa.

"Why don't we have a nice romantic dinner tomorrow night and you tell me all about the traditions you love. This year you can experience my traditions. Then next year, me and you decide on what traditions we want together." His words were so sweet and kind, my heart fluttered.

"That sounds really good, but I've got my weekly Euchre night with the girls. They're already mad I'm not doing our annual *White Christmas* movie. If I skip out on Euchre night, I might not have any friends when we get back from Chicago," I said.

"Okay. That's fine." He got out of the car. "Let's get this over with."

"Does that mean he's going to be around for a while?" Poppa asked.

"I hope so," I said back to Poppa before I got out of the Jeep with my bag in one hand and Duke trotting alongside of me.

"Right there." Poppa pointed to one of the windows of the outside of the funeral home.

"Yes. Right there you laid in corpse." It was something that I wrestled with every time I came to see Max, even on unrelated issues.

"You know that every Sims before me was right there in that window. You'll be there too." He tapped his temple. "Do you think if you asked Max, he'd agree to put a plaque up underneath that window with our name on it?"

"I don't think so. All the Harrisons have laid there, not to mention the Ramseys and Browns." It wasn't like we were special. "When there's no other competition in town and there's only a couple of windows where the casket will go, it's not that special." I muttered with my head looking down at the ground so Finn would think I was talking to Duke.

"Hhmmm." Poppa stood outside the window and looked at it like a shrine. Duke sat down next to Poppa.

The two-story brick home had been an old house that'd been transformed into the only funeral home in Cottonwood. There were two large, ceiling to floor windows in the front and our family had always been laid out in that one particular window.

"We better get in there because I'm limited on time." I

tapped my watch.

"Come on, Duke," I called when I got to the steps. He wasn't budging from sitting next to Poppa in front of that darn window. It looked as if Duke was paying some freaky homage to that window. "Come on," I called a little bit louder and clapped my hands together.

"Woooooo." Finn wiggled his fingers at me and did some sort of ghost call. "Maybe he sees one of them spirits you believe in."

"Stop it." I smacked his fingers away in a joking manner. He stepped inside the funeral home and I left Duke outside. It wasn't like he was going to go anywhere. Everyone around town knew Duke and he would find his way around the town or sit on the porch to wait for me.

We headed inside, and a chill swept over me. No matter how many times I'd come in here, and the fact that I actually had a relationship with a ghost, this place still gave me the heebie-jeebies. Going to the morgue wasn't at the top of the list of things I liked to do as Sheriff.

The morgue was in the basement. The upstairs of the funeral home was worlds different than the morgue. The funeral home had warm carpeting, richly painted walls, antique furniture and the large crown molding. The morgue had concrete floors, swinging metal doors and steel tables. The entire thing was just one big, cold room.

I looked through the small port window in the swinging doors that stood between me and Max. He was standing over Leighann's body.

I tapped my fingernail on the glass. Max's head jerked up and when he noticed me, he waved us in.

There was no denying that there was something so strange

and eerie when you were in the presences of the deceased all laid out in their Sunday best clothes.

Finn's shoulders shook, and he did a little jump in the air when we passed the first room on the left.

The sound of a drill and clink of metal told me that Max was hard at work.

"Are you going to be okay?" I asked Finn before we stepped into the room where I could see Max from the little port-hole window in the door.

"I'm fine." Finn's man-ego appeared, which was rare. "I saw Leighann yesterday. Like all the others."

Seeing a dead body at the scene was much different than on the table at the coroner's office, cracked wide open and with all sorts of tubes draining all that fluid.

"Good evening, Max," I said and pushed into the door with Finn behind me. I plucked a couple of gloves from the box and snapped them on my hands. I held the box out to Finn for him to get some. "Finn?" I waved a hand in front of his blank face. "You're white as a ghost."

I took a quick look around to see if Poppa was there and Finn had seen him.

"Finn!" Max dropped one of his metal instruments on the tray next to him and ran over, catching Finn right before his head smacked the floor. "Finn?"

Max shook him by the shoulders.

"I'm guessing he's still not used to being in a morgue," Max said with a bit of entertainment.

"Remember the reserve officers are pampered men of the law," I joked and grabbed the smelling salt for Max to crack open and swipe under Finn's nose. "Here," I took off my jacket, though I knew Max kept the temps in here nearly freezing, but poor Finn needed a pillow. "Wad this up and put it under his head. He'll be fine."

About that time something beeped. It was like a cow poker to Max's back-end, and he jumped. He almost dropped Finn's head on my flat coat.

"I've been waiting for this report." He scurried over to the fax machine. "I contacted Tom Geary last night and wanted to get his take on it."

"On what?" I asked and walked over to Leighann.

Finn had gotten to his feet and was drinking a glass of water Max had gotten for him.

Outside of the V cut Max had performed on her and the tubes draining out of her, she looked like she'd been sleeping. Her long red hair had dried since she had been pulled out of the river. It laid around her in long waves. The kind of waves women paid a lot of money to get from a fancy salon. I rested my hand on her hand that was lying at her side and said a little pray to myself. I noticed a small heart tattoo on the fatty part of the underside of her thumb.

"Leighann," I said as if she could hear me, which she might. I looked over at Poppa. "I'm going to find out exactly what happened." I promised the young girl then and there. "I want you to know that no daughter deserved the treatment you received."

I felt it necessary to apologize for her parents. If I'd know about how Sean treated her and Jilly, I'd probably have been more on Leighann's side during all the calls Sean had placed to the department to bring his daughter home and runaways she'd attempted. I'd certainly have arrested Sean for some sort of domestic violence abuse.

I even found myself mad at Jilly for not stepping up to the

plate and being a mother to the poor girl.

"Thank you, Tom." Max gripped the faxed papers and shook them in the air. "When I did the preliminary toxicology report on Leighann, there were some traces of Ambien in her system." He pulled out his file and opened it, pointing to all sorts of numbers on a grid that I didn't even understand.

Tom Geary was the owner of a lab in Clay's Ferry that I used in the department when I needed something fast.

"Sleeping pills?" I asked, not real sure. I continued to flip through the file to see the notes he'd made in the sidebars.

"Yes. Just a trace. Tom has some real sophisticated equipment that would help detect just exactly how much." He took the papers off the fax machine and muttered Tom's report under his breath. "Yep. I knew it."

"Did Tom confirm?" I wondered.

"He did. Which doesn't necessarily point to a homicide, but the amount in her system is just enough to put her in a deep sleep and if she was underwater, she wouldn't wake up." His eyes bore into my soul.

"Are you saying she didn't take them?" I asked and looked over at Finn. The color had come back into his face.

"I'm saying that the time of death doesn't coordinate with how long her body has been under the water." He beat around the bush.

"She was given the medication before her car went into the river," Poppa appeared next to Finn and he stood over him. "This boy needs to toughen up."

"Someone gave her the medication. When she had no control over her body, they put her in the SUV and somehow got it into the water." I was playing the game with Poppa without Max understanding what I was doing.

"Someone did give it to her, but how did they get the car in park? The SUV can roll if the keys aren't in it, but how did they get the car in park? Was someone in the car with her?" Poppa posed questions that were so hard to answer.

"Who could lift her into an SUV?" I asked.

"These are questions you're going to have to find the answers to." Max made another copy of Tom's report and stuck it in the file labeled "Sheriff's File" along with the case number of Leighann Graves. "The water in her lung tissue and the time release of the sleeping pills don't coordinate. There was some time in between."

"It's hard for me to forget the prescription bottle of Ambien for Sean Graves on their kitchen window sill." There was a light of uneasiness that passed between me and Max.

"Sean can be a bear. I know that. You know that he hangs out with me and some of the guys and plays cards, but I don't think he could kill that little girl of his. She gave him fits, but he loved her," Max said.

"He also hit his wife and daughter. Not only that, he also kicked his daughter out of the house, and she had to live in her SUV and got food from the food shelter at church." It almost made me sick that Max was almost making Sean Graves out to be a great man.

"He never said anything about all that." Max handed me the file. "I'm not saying he didn't give some of his sleeping pills to her either or that he did, but I am saying that it appears she had some sleeping pills. Now, whether she took them herself I can't tell you that, but I do know it's enough that if she was in a bathtub and went under, she'd not wake up."

I wasn't asking Max to do my job. I knew that he could only give me the facts based on what Leighann's body was telling him. It was now on my hands to take what her body had said along with the evidence I was collecting to arrest a suspect.

"Now, I don't know about what you found in the SUV, but I'm positive she didn't have time to put the keys in her pocket from the time of death to the length of time she was in the water."

"She was murdered," I said it out loud and declared it right there.

"I'll be out here." Finn got our attention and he pushed out the door.

"I'm sorry this has happened right here at Christmas. It seems the holiday season doesn't stop death from coming. I'm so busy, I feel like a spec of water in a hot skillet." Max untied the white apron from around his waist and threw it in the clothing basket and motioned for me to come to his office.

"I'd heard last night that you were full." I waited for him to get the paperwork together that I had to sign off on.

"Yep. Alright. I'm going to say this was a homicide because I just can't make the timeline work." He turned the piece of paper towards me and pushed it across the desk. "Sign right here."

I took one of the many pens from his pen cup and signed exactly where he told me to.

"I'll keep you posted if I find out anything else." Max stood up. There was a frown on his face. I could tell he was hurting because he trusted Sean just like the rest of us even though Sean hadn't been found guilty of anything.

"Looks like we've got us a killer and we better get jingling if we are going to figure it out before Christmas." I grabbed Finn's hand and dragged him out of the funeral home.

Chapter Nine

"Now where are we going?" Finn held onto the handle of the passenger side door when I peeled the Wagoneer off the curb after slamming the gearshift in DRIVE.

"According to Tom Geary's report." I tapped the copy of Max Bogus's report he'd put in the file he'd given me about Leighann Graves. "Leighann had Ambien in her system."

"So, she took a sleeping pill?" He asked with a peculiar look on his face.

"I don't know, but I think her car will have more evidence we can pull from and that's why I'm going to drive on out to Clay's Ferry to S&S Auto. Read the file to me." I knew we were racing against time because it was pretty darn close to any business closing up for the night.

Clay's Ferry was about twenty minutes away. The curvy roads were hard to navigate during a bright sunny day, much less a dark winter's evening with the temperature dropping rapidly. I gripped the wheel and listened to Finn read the initial report and Tom Geary's report sent by fax to Max.

"Max says here that the Ambien had been in her system and her nervous system long enough that she wouldn't be able to unbuckle her seatbelt, drive into the water, put the car in park and put the keys in her pocket. The timeline of the effects of the drug in Leighann's system doesn't add up. This is where he concludes it's a homicide." Finn closed the file and I could feel his stare.

"This is why I couldn't let Sean take her SUV to Graves Towing. We need to go over her car with a fine-tooth comb." There had to be some clues. "I doubt we'll get any prints off of it since the mud would act as sandpaper."

"When I initially looked at the car, I didn't see anything in there. There wasn't a purse, jacket or nothing. I've never seen a teenager's car so clean." Finn made a good point. "I thought it was strange and I did note it in the report."

"What about an emergency kit?" I asked. "Vividly I remember that Sean had mentioned that Leighann had an emergency kit in her car that included food, water and first aid when I went to their house on the initial phone call when they reported her missing."

"One with her initials on it, too." Poppa chimed in after he reappeared in the Jeep.

"You'd know it because it had her initials on it," I said.

"Not that an emergency kit that's monogramed should surprise me around here, but it does. Still. I didn't find anything in her car. Nothing." He shook his head. "I even looked under the seats." He reached over and flipped the heat up a notch. "It's getting colder. It does feel like snow weather."

"Don't even start with that," I warned. "I'm in no mood to hear about this ridiculous notion there's a blizzard coming."

"Wow, someone's on edge. I'd heard the holidays bring it out in everyone." He joked but I didn't laugh. "Listen," he reached over and put his hand on my shoulder. "This is just a job. We can't live every second and have every conversation built around the job, Kenni. We have to have a life outside of the office."

"We do. It's just that right now, we need to get to Leighann's car and figure out something." It was hard for me to put the job as second in my life. I'd never done or known anything in my adult life other than being the badge. It'd been a challenge for me to have a life outside of the office when I clearly wasn't used to it.

"I'm not saying we don't go and check out the car. It's pretty dark and it's not like the killer left a calling card. Really, this can wait until the morning." He was right, but I didn't care.

"Yep. See here." Poppa ghosted between us and he jabbed his finger in Finn's chest. Finn drew his hand up and rubbed the spot. "My Kenni-Bug is the sheriff. She calls the shots. You take them, Buddy."

"All I'm saying is that while it's fresh in our minds, we need to go look at the SUV. We have flashlights." I put the turn signal on when I got to the chain link fencing that was built around S&S Auto.

It was a first-class junk yard, tow company and impound lot. They had their cars stacked up in neat heaps and in rows of repose. The office hours posted reminded me that they closed at five p.m., something I'd forgotten.

"Says they're closed," Finn mentioned. "Like I said, we can come back tomorrow."

"Not closed if I see a light on." I noticed dots of lights coming out of a closed window blind from the far end of the building. I grabbed my bag and got out. "Somebody has got to be in there."

Instead of knocking on the door of the office, I walked up to the window and knocked on it. Two of the blinds snapped open and two beady eyes stared at me. I recognized those eyes as the secretary who gave me a hard way to go last time I needed a car out of their lot.

I gave her a minute to walk down to the door after she'd shut the blinds.

"You again." The woman's happiness to see me was apparent in her tone. "I'm assuming you're here for the girl's SUV?"

"Actually, I just need to look at it." I stared at her baby blue cardigan that was tucked down into the waist of her brown pleated pants. She still had the same chin length bob that looked more like a football helmet than style. "It's part of evidence and no one is going to move that car until I clear it."

"I'm in here finishing up the paperwork. If I can get ahold of Frank, I'll see what I can do." She started to pull the door shut. "And only because I feel bad about that girl and would like to get a murderer behind bars."

Finn looked down and scratched his head. His eyes peered at me from under his brows. "Why do you think this is a murder?" He asked her.

"Because the last time she was here," she flung a finger at me, "it was a murder. By the way she's acting and by the late hour of the night, it's gotta be a murder." She turned and went back into the office, shutting the door to keep us out in the cold.

There was a slight grin on his face.

"You sure did get her britches in a tangle last time we were here." He laughed.

"Look at him." Poppa pointed out. "He's pickin' up on our sayings."

That was two compliments for Finn tonight from Poppa in a Poppa kinda way. The funeral home window thing and now the Southern slang.

"You are a something else, Finn Vincent." I couldn't help but laugh back, then I got all serious again. "We are going to quickly just check out a few things. I'd like to get a good look to make sure there's no first aid kit in there with Leighann's initials. Or if the entire emergency kit is gone."

"Why does that seem so important to you?" He asked.

"The side panel of the car is gone. Did she take the emergency kit out at some point after she hit or was hit by whatever? Use it?" Then it dawned on me. My jaw dropped. "What if someone slipped her the pill and knew she'd drive somewhere, become unconscious and wreck?"

"She did wreck but didn't die." Finn looked out as though he were trying to piece the incident together.

"We need to determine how fast the car was going because if that's true, Max said that she didn't have any physical signs," I threw that out there because we had to put the facts with our theories so they would be a complete puzzle of what exactly happened.

"Do you think that someone followed her and finished off the job?" Finn asked.

"Exactly." Poppa clapped his hands and did a jig. "We need to find out where that panel has disappeared to. That is going to be the second crime scene in this murder."

"What's the first?" I asked.

"Wherever she was when someone slipped her the pill." Poppa's words left chills down my legs.

"What's first?" Finn asked with furrowed brows.

"Wherever the person slipped her the pill." I repeated Poppa and looked at Finn with furrowed brows. "I mean," I gulped and caught myself. "I think the scene we investigated at the river is the third crime scene. The first is the pill. The second is wherever that side panel is and the third is the river."

"We need to find that side panel." Finn ran his hands through his hair. He let out a long-exhausted sigh that hit the condensation of the cold air and a stream of smoke trailed. "You need a vacation. You say things out of nowhere like you're having your own little conversation. After we take a look at the SUV, if Frank is here, why don't you go home and go to sleep. Skip feeding the needy at church."

"Yes. A murder stresses me out, but I'm not skipping church tonight. It makes me feel good." I turned and gave Poppa the stare down. He was as sneaky as a pickpocket.

"I guess Frank is here," Finn said and pointed at the locked gate leading into the impound lot. The lights had turned on and Frank was standing there in the same outfit I'd seen him in every time I'd interacted with the man.

"Evening, Sheriff. Deputy." Frank unlocked the gate. "I've only got about fifteen minutes until I've got to scat. Wife duties and all."

"Thank you, Frank." It felt good to call him by his real name since I'd never known it. "It'll just take a few minutes tonight. Can't see much in the dark and we just wanted to check something out."

"No problem." He held the clipboard out for me to sign. I was glad to see they kept records because people were dishonest, and a killer would have no problem jumping this fence to mess with the evidence. "I'll tell you that whoever knocked this car's side panel off has to have some red on it." He took me around to the missing side panel of the car. "Right here's some strange marks. I noticed it when I was doing the checklist we have to do after we pick up a car to make sure the owner can't come back and say we did the damage."

Finn and I both unclipped our flashlights from the utility belt at the same time. I took a good look at the marks and made a note to take some photos of it when I got the camera out of my bag.

"I'll take the driver's side and you take the passenger side." I dragged the light from the front bumper, along the side, and ended at the back bumper. There didn't appear to be anything that struck me as unusual. I opened up the driver's side door and shined the light at the dashboard. There was a dried water line but nothing else. The floorboard was clean, and the driver's seat was too. A little too clean for me.

I reached into my bag and grabbed a pair of gloves and some fingerprint dusting powder to coat the seatbelt release button with.

"You're dusting for prints tonight?" Finn asked.

"Listen, if our theory about someone slipping Leighann a pill and hoping she'd wreck is true, they had to have gotten her out of her seatbelt. And a killer in a crime of heat, which appears to be what this is, doesn't think things through enough that they would put on gloves." I snapped gloves on my hands.

"It's also freezing out and it was the night she was found." Which was his way of saying the killer might've had on gloves.

"Exhaust all possibilities." I didn't have a good response for him. "I'm going to dust."

He eased back around to his side of the SUV but not without taking a pair of gloves from my bag.

"I'm going to look under all the seats really good now," he said while I brushed on the dust and let it settle. "You know that I can actually put my whole body into the space between the steering wheel and the seat."

This struck me as odd because Leighann and I were pretty much the same height and build. If I were driving or she were driving, the seat wouldn't've been back this far.

"What did you say?" Finn leaned into the passenger side front door and shined his flashlight in my face.

"Look." I got into the seat and extended my arms and feet out in front of me. Neither of them touched the wheel or the pedals. "The last person in this car was a good four to five inches taller than Leighann."

"Good work. Now you're using your noggin'." Poppa grinned from ear-to-ear in the back. "Which means that someone drove this car into the river, but how did they get out in time, turn the car off and put the keys in Leighann's pocket?"

"What am I missing?" I gnawed on the situation.

"I'm going to go look around." Poppa ghosted away.

"I hope you find something," I whispered under my breath.

"We are missing this side panel and where this murder started," Finn said with a long sigh.

"Did you see any emergency kit?" I asked and got back out of the car.

I reached down into my bag and got my camera out so I could take pictures of the seat and took my measuring tape out for some accurate measurements.

"There's nothing in here." Finn walked around and took the gloves off. "What about any fingerprints?" He leaned into the passenger side when I moved to write down the measurements.

"See any?" I asked.

"No. I'm afraid the grit in the river water must've acted like sandpaper like we thought." The glow of his flashlight circled inside of the SUV before he twisted around and shined it in my face.

"At least we got some information about how tall the killer might be." I looked at Finn's chilled eyes.

"What if she took the pills and was awake just enough to undo her seatbelt, push her seat back, drive the car enough in the water to carry it and pass out. Then she drowned." Finn was looking at all angles which he should've. But I was looking at my facts.

Poppa.

Chapter Ten

"I'm so glad you were still able to come." Preacher Bobby had greeted me at the doors of the undercroft.

"I don't leave for Chicago for a few days. I'd never miss this," I assured him and tried to switch hats from sheriff to volunteer. More times than not, this was a difficult task for me.

"I'm talking about taking time out of the investigation for Leighann Graves." His chin fell to his chest. "Bless her young soul."

My eyes darted back and forth wondering if I was supposed to let out a big amen, hallelujah, or a nod. I chose none of those and pinched a smile when he looked back up.

"I went by to see the Graves and they sure are having a real hard time and questioning God." Preacher Bobby rocked back on those black, preacher, thick-sole shoes and folded his hands in front of him. "I know I'm getting ahead of myself by a couple of weeks, but I sure do hope to see you more during Sunday service. It's been brought to my attention that you won't be at the annual tree lighting, caroling, and sleigh rides this year." He lifted his hands in the air and whispered something as he looked up to the sky.

"I'm super excited about Finn's parents' tradition on

Christmas eve. They go to a bar and tie one on before Santa comes." I winked, elbowed him and walked in the undercroft.

"Oh Kendrick Lowry, I never can tell when you're pulling my leg." He laughed behind me. "I'll see you in the new year," he called out.

I stuck my hand in the air and wiggled my finger as I continued to walk through the undercroft and followed the sounds of the bell choir.

"I'm not joking about this one," I confirmed about the Vincent's bar tradition.

Finn did tell me that they all went to a local pub, put down a couple of pints before they came home to do a sort of white elephant exchange. It was pretty exciting to get to see a new tradition.

There were a few minutes between the time I got there and the time the doors opened for supper, so I headed up the back steps of the undercroft to the foyer of the church that led into the sanctuary. The three Christmas trees lit up on the stage in front of where the congregation sits literally took my breath away. The trees were so full this year and I wondered where they'd purchased them. It kinda made me envious that I didn't get a tree, though I wasn't leaving until the day before Christmas Eve. Maybe I'd rethink getting one. At least I could enjoy it while I was here.

The poinsettia plants were strategically placed around the steps leading up to the stage where the bells were set up going down the center. The bell choir, which consisted of most of the Sweet Adeline's, was very special to Cottonwood and the church. There were bells of different shapes and sizes, each one of them making a different tone when played. Mama stood behind Lynn Bishop and appeared to be instructing her on how to handle the bell.

Lynn was the newest addition to the choir and I wasn't sure why she was holding Mama's bell. It was a job that Mama took very seriously.

"I'll never get tired of listening to the sweet sounds of those bells." Poppa appeared next to me, making me jump.

I glanced around to see if anyone saw me.

"Oh, I forgot." He made the motion that he had an imagery bell in his hand. "Ding, ding." He let out his boisterous laugh that was one thing I truly missed.

He was being a smart-alec. I'd once asked him to try and somehow announce himself before he just appeared because it freaked me out. Then he decided it was best to ding himself in like Clarence from the movie *It's a Wonderful Life*.

"You are far from an angel," I joked back to him underneath my breath. To me he was the only angel, but I didn't tell him that. His head was already big enough.

"Why doesn't your Mama have on her white gloves?" He asked a very good question.

The bells were very sensitive and had to be tuned every year. It was something that was set in the budget of the church because they had to be sent off for tuning. Each member of the bell choir had to wear gloves to be able to handle them with care. Mama was a stickler. Her gloves were washed after every practice and performance and to see her up there without the gloves and standing behind Lynn made me very curious.

"I swear it's you going away for Christmas that's put her in a funk and she just can't get out of it. I hope you're happy." Poppa ghosted up to Mama after he'd decided to skin me a new one.

When he placed a hand on her shoulder, I saw her look up

and smile. I wasn't sure if she felt him or it was the sweet sounds of the bells, but I took much more comfort in thinking she felt her father's presence.

She looked over at me and had that wonderful grin on her face. I returned it. She walked down the steps with her Southern ease and grace.

"Are you getting in your concert since you won't be here to hear the real thing?" She asked, referring to the Christmas tree lighting ceremony that ended with a bell choir performance and good food. "It's going to be real pretty too at the fairgrounds." She nodded.

This year the tree lighting and festivities, like Mama's pageant, were going to be the same night down at the fairgrounds.

"I'm here to do volunteering for the food shelter tonight and I couldn't stand not to come up here and watch you when I heard the bells." It was a very fond memory of my Mama dragging me to bell choir practice with her when I was a child.

It was the traditions that we Southern women loved the most and it was starting to sink in my gut that I was going to miss out on that, but quickly turned that thought into Finn and his family traditions. What was one year? No big deal. At least that's what I told myself.

"Your Poppa loved to hear the bell choir." She shivered. "I swear every time I pick up that bell, I feel him."

"Why aren't you playing your bells?" I questioned and ignored the fact that Poppa was still standing there and how much so Mama was right.

"I can't be crowned Snow Queen and come play the bells in the same night." She did that wave thing with her hand. I pushed it down. "My nails have got to have plenty of time to dry before I take the crown...er...participate in Snow Queen. Those gloves fit so tight, I just can't risk it."

"That's disturbing." I sucked in a deep breath.

"Anyways, since I'll be moving around the tree lighting talking to everyone, I figured I better step down this year and let Lynn get the hang of it." She looked up at Lynn and squinted when she planted a fake smile across her face. "Bless her pea-pickin' heart. She just ain't got no rhythm."

"At least she's trying." I assured her. "And you've got a few days until the event, so I'm sure she'll be practicing until then."

"Hhmmm." Mama rolled her eyes. "I'm not so sure about that. Them youngins' of hers are so excited about Christmas, she said they haven't slept a wink. Of course, Vernon's not. He told her that he was the one who had to go to work in the morning and how she got to stay at home and take a nap." Mama's nostrils flared. "You know what I'da told your daddy if he said that to me?"

"No, and I don't want to know." My dad was a saint and I just knew there was a crown filled with jewels in heaven with his name on it because Vivian Sims Lowry was one hard woman to deal with.

"I'm gonna tell you anyways, because this is a life lesson for you." She poked me in the arm with her finger nail. I rubbed out the pain and prepared myself to just let whatever it was she had to say roll right on over me.

"Mama, you stop that carryin' on, you hear me?" I swallowed. "Daddy never had the nerve to try and tell you what to do."

"That's because I laid down the law when we were dating." She gave me the good ole, hard Baptist nod. "With you going away and all for Christmas, you apparently haven't laid down the law with Finn."

"Mama, that's enough," I warned. "Or I'll be gone every year at Christmas."

"You're gonna miss me when I'm dead and gone." Her eyes snapped at me. "And regret doing me this way."

"I love you and you know that." I gave her a hug even though she was pouting. "Anyways, I better let you get back to your teaching."

"Toodles." Mama waved and headed back up to the stage. She did a few nods and smiles at Lynn before I headed back down to the undercroft where all the volunteers had started to gather around who else...Betty Murphy.

Out of the corner of her eye, Betty noticed I'd come into the room and she quickly straightened up and shut her mouth.

Everyone turned to see me and scattered in all sorts of directions. I swear it was the uniform. If I'd put on street clothes, they would've stood there and gossiped just like they do when we have our weekly Euchre girl's night out. It was the same when I went to talk to someone about a case. I guarantee that if I went to see Juanita Liberty tomorrow without the uniform on, she'd be a lot more forthcoming and it was truly something for me to think about.

"I'm thinking y'all weren't talking about the upcoming weather?" I asked Betty.

"Heck no. You know what we were talking about. I told you about it before I left work." She and I both walked over to get the tablecloths, so we could put them on each table. It was sorta our job each year. For some reason, they'd stuck us on the committee that set the tables and cleaned up. I'd much rather been serving the food, but that job was given to the women of the church who do a little ministering to the homeless.

"Did you hear anything I should know about?" I asked, referring to any gossip.

"Well, I'd heard, hearsay," hearsay was a nice way of saying gossip. "Angela Durst had taken Leighann under her wings over the last couple of months. In fact, when Leighann and Manuel had come in here to get a warm meal a few weeks ago, Angela was curious to why they were there and Leighann told her everything about how her daddy had kicked them out. Sean Graves abused her. Now everyone in here thinks he's a killer."

"Is that right?" I asked and tugged on the edge of my side of the table cloth while she tugged on her side before we slipped it on the first table.

"Mmmhhh," she ho-hummed. "What do you think about that?" Her jaw dropped. "You already knew about that, didn't you?"

I tapped my five-star sheriff's badge on my pocket.

"I wasn't elected for my good looks," I joked because I never wore my hair out of my ponytail or wore makeup during the day.

"My stars." She gasped. "Are you telling me that when I go to work in the mornin', Sean Graves is going to be sitting in our cell?"

"Did I say that?" I asked. "Now that's how rumors get started."

"You didn't say it and I've worked with you long enough to read you a little better than you want me to." Her face shifted to the side and she looked over at me out of the corner of her eye.

"I can't believe that Angela Durst didn't know about it since she's Sean's secretary and all," I said knowing that I really needed to put Angela at the top of my list to talk to.

"What if Angela said something to Sean that next day and he laid into Leighann for saying something about their home life?" Poppa appeared next to us.

I avoided his stare since I knew everyone was looking at me. I had to play it cool.

"You and I both know that something fishy happened." She grabbed another table cloth and handed an edge to me.

Over the next few minutes we did our little ritual of putting on the table cloths together. It wasn't until we went our separate ways where she did the napkins while I did the cups that I got lost into my train of thought.

Poppa followed me around, giving little tidbits of information and how I needed to question anyone and everyone.

"While you and Finn were playing detective, I went down to the river." Apparently, that's where Poppa ghosted off to while I was at S&S Auto. "I walked along the banks."

"Walked?" I questioned him and looked down at his feet.

"More like swept?"

"It is quicker," he assured me. "You know that Sterling Stinnett has a lot of stuff down there."

"It's cold out. He's got to be staying at the shelter." I'd bent down and acted like I was picking something off the floor, so no one would hear or see me talking to what they'd think was myself. "I hate to admit it, but it's too cold out there for a frog, much less a person."

"Sterling still goes and checks on his stuff. I saw him. He might've heard something." Poppa wagged his thick finger at me. "No stone unturned. Haven't I told you that before?"

"On more than one occasion." I stood back up and looked over at Betty. "I learned that motto from you," I said to him with some pride.

Had Angela really taken in Leighann? I wondered why Manuel didn't follow suit. Where was that car panel? I couldn't help but wonder what that fight was about this time last night at the Christmas dance.

These were all sorts of questions that I needed answered and the only way to do it was to go and talk to Angela. Making another little visit to Manuel wouldn't hurt either.

As if God himself gave me a sign, because we were in his holy house, Sterling Stinnett was the first to walk into the undercroft doors. His eyes met mine and I could tell he had something to say.

"Give me an extra helping of mashed potatoes," I told Viola White who was on mashed potato duty.

"As long as you vote for me for Snow Queen." Her eyes drew down her nose. Her hand lifted to pat the fur stole neatly draped over her shoulders. The circular diamond pin held the ends together.

"It's for Sterling," I said flatly and looked at her fur. "Now don't you go playing Mama's games," I warned her in a loud voice so Mama would hear. "Nothing good can come from that."

"Hush your mouth, Kendrick Lowry." Mama took a spoonful of green beans and put them on my plate. "You can vote for Viola. It's not going to help her none."

"Mmhhhmmm," Viola's lips pinched. "We'll see."

"What's that supposed to mean?" Mama dropped the serving spoon in the tray of green beans. "You better back up your words, Viola White."

"Ain't we pickin' our peaches before they're all fuzzed up?" Viola was getting all sorts of sassy with Mama. She scooped up another spoon of mashed potatoes and served them on top of the others she put on my plate.

"Ladies, this is no way for a future Snow Queen to act. Especially in the Lord's house." I simply used their guilt techniques on them. "God don't like ugly."

"You sure are right." Mama's shoulders straightened. She picked up the serving spoon and went back to the line that'd now formed out the door.

Two things Southern women loved: God and food. We were right here amongst both and I used them against the pair who took their heritage more than most.

I turned around with my tray to see if I could find Sterling.

I didn't have to look around too much. Sterling was already through the line and sitting alone at a table up front.

"Hey, Sterling," I greeted him and sat down, putting the plate on the table.

"Sheriff." He nodded and sopped up what was left of the gravy with his biscuit. "Getting cold out there."

"It sure is." I pushed my plate towards him.

His face jerked upwards.

"I'm not hungry," I said building up to my questioning. "I've got this murder investigation on my mind and just not able to really eat."

I never understood why Sterling had chosen to live the life he did. He was talented in many construction type jobs and never was at a lack of job offers. He just chose to not have a house or any sort of living quarters. As long as he wasn't a menace to Cottonwood, he didn't bother me any.

"I know that you're the unofficial eyes and ears of Cottonwood and you've really given me some great information over the years in a lot of my investigations." I wanted to stroke his ego a little while he stuffed his face. It was true. He blended in so much that he'd become part of the landscape. People never really noticed he was around.

"I'd heard you found that girl down at the river." He folded the turkey slice in half and stuffed it in his mouth.

"I'm thinking it was right around where you hang out. Though I know it was cold that night and I'm sure you weren't there, but if you did hear something that I might need to know, you know where to find me." I stood up. "I hope you have a very Merry Christmas."

"Sheriff," Sterling called after me. He waved me over. "I did hear something that night but I didn't go check it out because I heard tires."

"You heard tires?" I asked.

"You know that hairpin turn about a mile before Chimney Rock put in?" He asked. I nodded. "I heard a crash. No squealing tires or nothing. But there was another car behind it that stopped."

"Did you see it?" I asked.

"No. I just heard it and didn't bother going to check it out when I heard the other car. I'm assuming they were there to help." His bushy brows furrowed.

"Help? Yeah, help kill," Poppa chimed in.

"Did you hear any voice?" I asked.

"No. Just tires of another car. A door slammed a few times and drove off again. I went back to getting some stuff together because it was the first night the shelter opened. But it didn't open until eleven thirty." He gave me a time.

"Eleven thirty." Poppa noodle the time as well as I did.

"Eleven thirty," I repeated.

"It was about fifteen minutes later that the tow truck came." He stopped me in my tracks.

"Did you say tow truck?" Poppa and I asked at the exact same time.

"I know it was a tow truck because the rotating round lights was exactly what I needed to help find some of the items I wanted to take with me while I stayed in the shelter." He'd just given us a major clue.

"Did you see them?" I asked.

"No, I told you that I was getting my stuff together." He dragged the small plate with a piece of pie closer to him.

"Manuel, Jilly, and Sean drive the two trucks," Poppa named off my list of suspects.

"Thanks, Sterling. If you hear or remember anything else, can you call me?" I asked.

"Sure thing, Sheriff." He forked the pie and stuffed it in his mouth.

"Someone used the tow truck to toss her SUV in the river," Poppa said as his ghost kept up with me while I hurried around and picked up used paper plates and napkins.

My duty was clean up. Clean up more ways than one. I had a murder to clean up and it took everything I had not to run out of there and force my way into Graves Towing, giving Sean Graves a piece of my mind.

The more I cleaned, the more my mind wandered over the clues.

He had the bottle of Ambien. No matter how much he said he'd accepted Leighann and Manuel's relationship, he still loathed them together and it was apparent on his face when I'd seen him that night at the dance. Then there was his abusive side that I'd uncovered while talking to him and Jilly. He knew all of Leighann and Manuel's hook up places, Chimney Rock being one of them. He and Jilly left before Leighann. Leighann had plenty of time to make it home, talk to her parents, get slipped an Ambien before she was going to Chimney Rock to meet Manuel. Her father followed her and when she fell asleep at the wheel, he towed her car into the river and that's why the seat was set back, Leighann unbuckled, with the keys in her pocket.

But did Sean Graves really kill his own daughter? If he didn't, who lured her there?

Chapter Eleven

I barely felt like I'd slept when the alarm went off. Duke jumped off the bed, which meant he wasn't going to last through a snooze, so I rolled over and sat up in bed. The first thing on my mind was Leighann Graves and what I had to do today.

The warmth of my slippers felt so good as I padded out of my bedroom and down the hall towards the back door where Duke was eagerly paw dancing to be let out. This was the usual activity after he'd spent some time with Finn, alone, the night before. Finn wasn't aware of a treat limit and gave Duke a fistful of doggie biscuits.

I flipped on the coffee pot and unlocked the door, pushing open the screen door that stood between Duke and my fenced-in back yard. He darted out, yelping his way back to the fence where he smelled whatever critters had gotten into the yard while he was sleeping. He didn't care that the temperature had dropped a good twenty degrees overnight.

I shook my head and checked the coffee pot on my way back to the bathroom to start my hot shower. Duke took just enough time to smell and do his business while I got my shower.

While the hot water felt good, it still wasn't enough to make me feel confident that Sean Graves was who had killed

Leighann. The muffles and rumblings I'd heard around town, Sean Graves was already tried and arrested, and it wasn't a big secret he was known as a hard man.

It amazed me how something like news of a break-up took precedent over an abusive man, which would be this case. Because I'd never heard until this week that Sean was abusive.

The clues surely did point to him. I didn't have enough concrete evidence to arrest him. No judge or prosecutor would take a case on hearsay, gossip, and a bottle of Ambien. Not even the knowledge that he abused Leighann and Jilly, even that didn't make him a killer. Especially since Jilly or Leighann never filed a complaint.

I had to go see Rachel Palmer, Leighann's friend, while she was home from college. Heading to the tree lot to interview Juanita's boys was also on my list. The number one thing on my list was to check out the hair-pin curve Sterling Stinnett had told me about. There was no sense in wasting my time searching the area he was talking about without him. Having him there would shave off some time.

I'd decided to go with the street clothes today because I really was going to use my theory on Juanita and her boys to see if I could get some information out of them.

"Hello?" Finn's voice echoed down my hall while I was in my room getting ready. His voiced was followed up with Duke's nails tapping on the hardwood floor coming towards me.

"Hi," I stuck my wet head out the door and looked down the hall at Finn. "I'm going to throw my hair up in a ponytail. Fix yourself a cup of coffee."

My house on Free Row was small. It was a basic ranch with the family room in the front, kitchen in the back, small hall with two bedrooms and a bath. Off the kitchen was a small slab porch where I had a couple of chairs and premade fire pit. The chain link fence was great for Duke and Mrs. Brown, my neighbor, was nosy. It was a typical small-town neighborhood. Perfect for me since I'd spent a lot of my childhood here since it was my Poppa's house.

"No snow yet." Finn handed me a cup of steaming coffee and we clinked them together.

"No mentioning the 'S' word." I wasn't going to say or even think about snow until after we were on the big plane to Chicago. I'd welcome the snow there.

"Deal." He smiled and gave me a kiss on the head. "But you could use a little Christmas cheer around here."

"I was thinking about a Christmas tree since I do need to go to the Christmas lot today." I took a nice long sip of coffee and stared at him from underneath my brow. "I miss not having it in front of the window this year. It was fun to come home to."

"Just because we won't be here for Christmas eve and day, doesn't mean you can't celebrate while we are here. It's still the season." He always made so much sense. "Maybe after your Euchre girl's night out, I can walk over and we can decorate it."

"I'm a lucky girl." I walked over and gave him a sweet good morning kiss. "I guess I hate to get Mama's hopes up so when she does barge in here, she'd get the impression that I'd decided not to go to Chicago. I'll think about the tree."

She always came unannounced, which was typical of how a small town operates.

"Okay. Any word overnight or was everything quiet?" He asked.

"Not a word." I set my cup down and strapped my holster on underneath the grey sweatshirt I'd decided to wear with my jeans and duck boots. "Last night Sterling Stinnett told me that the night Leighann died, he heard a car crash about a mile away from Chimney Rock. That's just the beginning." My brows rose. "He also said that he heard another car come up right behind the crash. After a while, he saw swirling orange lights like a tow truck."

"You're just telling me this?" He looked at me with hawk eyes. "Let's go."

"Whoa. You just got here." I had to remind myself that we were having a friendly conversation and he wasn't trying to be my boss, which was difficult for me. "I think we need to pick up Sterling this morning from the shelter and take him to where he heard the sound. If it was Leighann, maybe the back panel is there."

"The tow truck? Sean?" Finn's jaw tensed. "I swear. If he hurt his daughter." He shook his head and stopped himself.

"I'm disturbed by the fight between the Graves and Libertys. Even if they didn't have anything to do with Leighann's death, they need to be reminded that gun slinging isn't on the up and up with the law. Which is why I still want to stop by the tree lot."

"I'm coming with you today since we've got Scott at the department." Finn grabbed two of my thermal mugs out of the cabinet and filled them up.

"You're going to have to go change because..." I opened the cabinet underneath my sink to fill Duke's bowl with kibble.

"Your theory." Finn laughed and headed to the back door. He grabbed my keys. "I'll meet you in the Jeep. I'll start it up. It's freezing out."

While Duke ate up his food, I gathered the rest of my stuff and even stuck a uniform in my bag just in case I decided to change while at the office today. With me wearing street clothes,

I didn't have to come home and change before Euchre tonight. I could work right up until it was time to go. Plus, there was food at Euchre because all the Sweet Adelines brought their best recipes.

"Did he say it was freezing out?" I questioned, eyeballing the grey sky that was starting to waken the day. "Not today," I said out loud to ward off any bad weather. "We've got a murder to solve."

I grabbed my bag and locked the back door, whistling for Duke to follow me out the gate.

"That didn't take long." I jumped into the driver's seat when I noticed Finn was already in the Jeep. He only lived a couple of doors down which made it nice for long date nights.

"I kept on the same pants but threw on a sweater." He unzipped his coat and showed me the black V-neck he'd chosen. "I hope your theory about how wearing street clothes is less intimidating than my gun because I can tell you that a gun speaks for itself."

"I've got my gun, it's the badge that scares them." I put the shift in reverse and then drive to head towards the south end of town where the shelter was located.

It was on the same road that we took to get to the fairgrounds, but it was still too early to go there. Not much was open in Cottonwood at seven a.m.

"You stay," I instructed Duke after we pulled into the shelter house and parked. "Ready?"

"I sure am." Finn opened his door and got out. I grabbed one of those peel off sheriff stickers I gave to children and stuck it in my back pocket against my phone.

The inside of the shelter house had a desk in the middle when you walked in. It was an old school that'd been converted into a men's and women's shelter. It was also a place where the child services and handicap services had started to work out of. The second floor was where the social security administration worked out of and I recognized a few of my neighbors.

"Hey there, Merv." I greeted the older man at the counter. He'd been a junk man as long as I'd been alive. He drove an old, beat up truck that was loaded to the gills with junk. It was probably a hazard to drive behind him not only because the stuff could fall right off and make you crash, but also because of the fact that he drove so slow that it took three times as long to drive down Main Street as normal. Either way, he was safe and warm here.

"Sheriff." He nodded. "What can I do you for?"

"Are you working the desk this morning?" I asked.

"Yes, ma'am." His chin drew a line up and down.

"Is Sterling Stinnett still here?" I asked.

"Is he in trouble?" He asked with a curious look on his face.

"Sterling? Absolutely not." I smiled.

"Then he's here. I'll go round him up." Merv got up from the chair and scooted his feet along the old school tile floor on his way back through the men's swinging door.

Finn and I stood silent while we waited, giving each other a look every time the door opened, and it wasn't Sterling. Finally, Merv and Sterling walked out.

"Sheriff." Sterling looked as if he'd just woken up. His disheveled hair still looked the same, but his eyes were tired. "Is something wrong?"

"Actually, do you remember when you helped me out at Viola White's Jewelry store a year ago?" I pulled out the sticker from my pocket. "I need you again."

A year or so ago, Sterling had stood in front of the jewelry store because it was just me and Betty holding down the fort. All he really had to do was to make sure no one would enter the store and trust me, Sterling was a little scary to most people who didn't know his good heart, so he was perfect to stand there for an hour.

"Are you kidding?" His eyes grew wide open as they locked on the sticker.

"May I do the honor?" I peeled the sticker off the backing and held it out to him.

"Yes, ma'am." He nodded and stuck his chest out real far. I patted the sticker right over his heart on his jacket.

"Afterwards, we are taking you out to breakfast at Ben's." I winked and gestured for him to follow us.

"Where we going?" he asked when we got into the Jeep. Duke jumped all around him and nudged Sterling's hand.

"Last night at the church you told me that you heard a car crash on the hairpin turn about a mile from Chimney Rock. I want you to show me where you think that crash occurred." I adjusted my rear-view mirror to look at him as I turned the Jeep towards the old river road.

He did the usual way everyone told directions.

"Take a left over the rickety bridge, at the wooden cross go right, go left at the fork, when you pass the old red barn with the chipped-up fence line, you're going to veer right. The hairpin curve is yonder." He pointed into the front seat.

Above the trees on the horizon rose a blurred and blood-red sun. The trickle of the dawn danced along the bare limbs of the winter trees and over the river.

"I'm going to pull along the side and put my flashers on so if there is something here, we don't disturb the evidence." I veered off the main part of the road and hugged the edge of the grass as close as I could, so I wouldn't get into the grass.

"You'd think there'd be some tire tracks." Finn looked out the window.

"Like I said, I heard a crash but no screeching tires," Sterling said before he got out of the car. "Just beyond that tree line yonder is where I set up camp. It's for that reason only." He pointed to the painted sky.

"It's beautiful." Finn's eyes had a look of awe as he turned his head from right to left, taking in all the amazing wonder. "We just don't have this type of sky in Chicago. I don't know if I'll take this for granted."

"I'm glad, but right now, we are here for the sound Sterling heard." I had to bring them back to the moment.

"If you thinks that's pretty, you should come stay at my camp sometimes when it gets pretty. Some people don't understand why I like to live out here. I don't understand why they want to stay cooped up inside when all the beauty is here." Sterling made perfect sense and that really made me respect him.

Finn looked at me and smiled. I smiled back.

We all took time to scour the area. The grass had become stiff from the cold weather. There didn't appear to be any car tracks. None of the tree trunks seemed to be disturbed or scratched as if a car had swung around and hit them.

"Hello!" I'd lifted my chin and hollered out into the quiet morning air.

Hello, ello, llo, ooo, the echo of my voice came back to me.

"Hi," Sterling said back to me.

"If there was a crash, it might've echoed," Finn said, knowing exactly what I was doing.

"That means that it could be a little more this way." I

pointed and walked a little further down. "Or even this way." I pointed behind me. "Either way, we know it's somewhere close if Sterling saw the lights of a tow truck."

"I'll go this way." Finn proceeded to walk opposite of me.

"Or over here." Poppa's ghost appeared across the road where the tree line was much closer to the road. "Because I think this here is a back panel."

I took off running across the road, not playing it off cool at all.

"Finn! Here!" I yelled making it half-way across.

He bolted towards me.

"It's definitely Leighann's side panel." Poppa stood with his hands down to his side.

The piece of plastic laid upside down and appeared to be the exact same color and shape as what was missing from Leighann's SUV.

"How on earth did you see this from over there?" Finn ran his hands through his hair before he bent down to look at it.

"I've got pretty good eyes." I gulped and sucked in a deep breath before I walked a little further away from the piece of car. "Here are some tracks."

There were tracks that showed tires had gone off the road and the back tire swiveled knocking into a tree, but not enough to make much damage to the tree.

"She wasn't going very fast." Poppa looked back towards the hairpin curve.

"She was either passed out or passing out. Let her foot up off the gas and didn't make the turn. The car probably wasn't going very fast. Just enough to smack the tree, knock off the panel." I pointed out.

"The echo must've made it sound much worse to Sterling

than it really was," Finn made a good point.

I took my phone out of my pocket and noticed the time. Betty should be in the dispatch and I quickly dialed the office.

"Sheriff's department," she answered.

"Betty, it's Kenni." I'd left the walkie-talkie at home so she didn't know it was going to be me.

"Mornin'. Where are you?" She asked.

"I'm out at Leighann's crash site. I'll fill you in on the details later. Is Deputy Scott there?" I asked.

"He is," she answered.

"Can you tell him to come back out here? I'd like him to tape off the crime scene while Finn and I go check out some other leads." It was nice having another set of hands so Finn and I could keep our heads together to keep working.

"Will do." She clicked off.

While we waited for Scott to get there, I took pictures and picked up the panel for the evidence. I also gave S&S Auto a call.

"S&S Auto." The secretary answered.

"Hi there, this is Sheriff Lowry from Cottonwood." I was met with silence. "I wanted to know if you could tell me if your tow company had a call about eleven thirty p.m. to Cottonwood about three nights ago?"

"Is this about that SUV you had Frank tow?" She asked. Though I knew it was more out of curiosity, I figured I'd be nice and see if she'd give me the information instead of me having to get a subpoena.

"Yes. I found that side panel that's missing and someone told me they saw a tow truck here and I wanted to check with you before I check with tows around here." The sound of a car about to go around the curve caught my attention.

"We didn't. The only call we've gotten from Cottonwood

this week was from you," she said through background noise of ruffling papers. "I hope that helps."

"More than you know." I clicked off and put my phone back into my pocket. "She said no," I said to Finn as we walked towards Scott's car.

"Are you thinking what I'm thinking?" Finn choked out the words that were swirling in my thoughts.

"Yes. That sonofabit..." Poppa started to go off on Sean Graves, but I gave him the look.

"I'm sickened at the thought. But we need more than just this." It wasn't enough. I knew it in my gut that something wasn't right.

In the beginning of me seeing Poppa, it was enough that I found the killer and he'd disappear back to wherever he'd been in the afterlife. The past few times, he'd sorta hung around until the killer was behind bars.

After Finn and Scott had a brief discussion about how we liked the crime scene to get taped off and how we liked the evidence bagged if he found some, we were back in the Jeep with Sterling and Duke on our way back to town.

"I'm starving." Sterling rubbed his hands together and down Duke. "It's so cold out there."

"It sure is." I flipped on the radio to keep me from discussing the situation with Finn. It was official sheriff business and it wasn't appropriate to talk in front of Sterling.

"Brrrr, it's cold out there." DJ Nelly's voice made my skin crawl. "The temperatures are dropping and making it ripe for the blizzard that's still set to move in a few days before Christmas. I hear that Dixon's Foodtown just got a new supply of shovels and sleds. Something for everyone." She laughed like she was taunting me through the radio. "Be sure you're ready for the storm of the century. Remember you can tune in here for all the storm updates while singing to your favorite carols on WCKK, Cottonwood's only radio station,"

"She just gets on your nerves, doesn't she?" Finn asked with a coy look across his face. He busted out laughing and bee-bopped his head when "Frosty the Snowman" came on and poked me with his finger in my rib making me laugh.

"No. It's just that it's my luck that this storm will happen. Trust me." I gripped the wheel and turned into the open parking space on Main Street right in front of Ben's Diner. "If we didn't have a big trip planned, there wouldn't be nary a snowflake."

"It's gonna snow," Sterling said as matter-of-factly as anyone could. "I've lived most my life outside and in many winters. The air feels different." He continued to talk and talk about the air as we sat down in one of the diner's tables near the front window.

"Flip your cups," Ben Harrison, owner of the diner that was his namesake, instructed with a pot of coffee in his hand. Not just any pot like those black plastic ones, it was the glass carafe that sat in the coffee pot itself. It was full to the brim.

"Keep it coming." Sterling nodded and licked his lips. "It's on the sheriff today."

"Is that right?" Ben grinned, showing off those cute dimples.

"Mmmhhhh. Sterling has been a big help this morning." I nudged Finn who'd sat down next to me. "Ain't that right, Finn?"

"Sure is," Finn confirmed.

Ben pulled the pencil out from behind his ear.

"Do you know what you want?" He asked.

"I want you to put in an order of a big heat wave." I joked

and turned when I heard the bell over the diner door ring.

"He makes a lot of things around here, but no way in hell is he going to cook up some warm weather." Ruby Smith's orange-lined lips were flapping, and she rubbed her elbow. "My elbow can tell weather better than any meteorologist and I'm telling you right here and right now, there's a blizzard a-coming."

"You heard it here first." Ben pointed to Ruby, who'd already moseyed on by and continued to rub her elbow up to the counter where she eased down into a stool. "Now, what do y'all want?"

"I'm gonna eat four pancakes, side of bacon, couple of biscuits and some fried eggs." Sterling truly didn't hold back.

"I'll have that too if it's on Kenni," Finn said with a twinkle in his eye.

"Make it three. When in Rome." I smiled.

Chapter Twelve

"This seems to turn our plans around today." Finn clicked his seatbelt in place after we'd taken Sterling back to the shelter, so he could get on with his day with his full belly.

"When is he going to learn that in the south, you're supposed to respect your elders? And by right," Poppa was perched on the edge of the backseat with his head stuck up between me and Finn like Duke did. "This is my Jeep and if you're driving, which I love, then I should be right up front."

My eyes stayed focused on the street, but my mind drifted off to how I was going to handle Sean Graves when I did announce he was our number one suspect.

"Do you want me to get Sean Graves and bring him in?" Finn asked like he was reading my mind.

"He does seem like the obvious suspect," Poppa said. "In case he lost his temper and maybe hurt the girl. Does he have a spare key to her SUV?"

"You know," I couldn't believe that I didn't think of that. "I do want you to go out and interview them. I want them interviewed separately." I wasn't sure if Jilly would be able to talk freely with Sean there. "You know what," I changed my mind. "Why don't you go out and interview them. I'll get Jilly alone at some point within the next day or two, but I really want to go to see Rachel Palmer."

"Sounds good." Finn shook his head. "I hate to say it, but since Sean admitted to hitting his wife and daughter, I see him in a different mirror. One that's not favorable."

"Darn right it's not favorable. Favorable? What kinda word is that?" Poppa spat. "Is that one of them northern words?" Poppa exaggerated northern so he'd get his point across that he listened to me earlier.

"I really wished I'd known this last year when we continued to take Leighann back to her house." I'd never regretted anything in my line of duty since I'd been sheriff, not even when I'd accused or arrested someone wrongly, but this time, I wasn't sure how I was going to forgive myself if Sean did kill Leighann.

Continuously, I took her back to her parents. I put her back in the danger she was apparently trying to get out of but didn't have the self-confidence to tell me. There was no sense in beating myself up about it. The only thing I could do was to get her murder solved and put whoever did it in jail for a long time. Even if it was Sean Graves.

When I'd dropped Finn off at the station, I stopped in real fast to update the white board.

I used the dry eraser to wipe off girl from dance and replaced it with Rachel's name. Not that she was a suspect, but she was one I wanted to question.

"Can you get me the address for the Palmer girl?" I tapped the tip of the dry-erase marker on the board.

"I sure can." Betty quickly flipped through her rolodex on her desk.

She loved to use that old thing and refused to even think about using the computer. Just like I wasn't about to go to a more modern way of communicating to Betty. The walkie-talkie system worked well and it was one of the things I didn't let Finn change when he wanted to bring the department up to the technology standards.

Next to Juanita's name, I wrote down the feud details between them and the Graves. Under Sean's name, I wrote down Sterling's information about the tow truck as well as the prescription medication. Under Leighann's name at the top, I made bullet points and wrote down the basics from Max's report.

Betty would gasp with each stroke of my marker since I'd not fully told her the details.

"Just terrible," she tsked and tried to act as though she wasn't paying too much attention. "Here you go." She handed me a piece of paper with the Palmers' address. I stuck it in my pocket.

"I'm heading out to the tree lot first. If you need me, just call me because I don't have my walkie-talkie with me." I gestured to Duke, he was cuddled up on his dog bed. "Do you mind?"

"Of course, I don't." Betty went back to filing and I headed out.

On my way out to the fairground, I took the opportunity to give the Palmer girl a call.

"Hi there, this is Sheriff Lowry and I'm looking for Rachel," I said to the woman who answered the other end of the phone.

"This is Cara, Rachel's mom. Is she in trouble?" There was a nervousness to her voice.

"No, ma'am." I put her at ease right off the bat. "I was going to stop by and talk to her about Leighann Graves."

"Poor Jilly," Cara's tone turned from fright to empathy. "I

just can't believe it. When I told Rachel this morning, she was stunned."

"I'd witnessed Rachel and Leighann in a little argument the other night, and I'd like to talk to her about it." Even though I knew I didn't need Cara's permission to talk to her daughter since Rachel was eighteen, I still had enough respect that it was necessary on my part.

"Rachel had nothing to do with Leighann's death," Cara made sure I understood that. "She was at home with me and her father after the dance. She told us about the fight."

"I just want to talk to her. Is she home?" I asked, wondering if I was going to have to change my plans this morning and stop by there first, then the fairgrounds.

"She's not here right now, but do we need a lawyer?" She asked with concern.

"I'm just going to ask her about Leighann and what she was like since they were best friends. Can you tell me when she'll be home?" I asked.

"She's volunteering for her old cheerleading team at the tree lot at the fairgrounds," she told me.

"Oh, I'm on my way there now. I'm going to ask her a few questions, but if you'd like to be present, I'll wait," I gave her the option.

"I'm fine with it as long as you don't think Rachel had anything to do with Leighann's death because she didn't."

"I have a few more questions." I wasn't about to back myself into the corner. I would have no idea until I talked to the girl if she led me to believe that she had anything to do with Leighann's murder. The only thing I knew was that there was a fight and I wanted to exhaust all possibilities of other killers before I arrested Sean Graves. I wouldn't know that until I talked to her.

The fairground was deep in the country off Poplar Hollow Road. We had our annual summer fair there when the carnival came to town. The 4-H club used it for their cattle shows as well, and the Boy and Girl Scouts used it for their camping excursions. There were barns and stalls used for any sort of livestock and there was even a stage under covering where the annual Miss Cottonwood Beauty Pageant was held during the summer.

It was also used for the local Farmer's Market as well as the tree lot for the Cottonwood High School, which made me believe that there was no better time to check out what the team thought of Manuel. Just out of curiosity, of course.

I was actually surprised to see that there were a lot of vendors set up under the big tent already.

The church choir members stood next to the concrete fire pit with their red cloaks and mittens, both lined in white fur. They were in harmony and peered down at their song books.

It appeared Cottonwood was going all out for this Christmas season. Figured, since I wasn't going to be here.

"One, two, three." There was a voice over the loud speaker. I turned to see a man with a microphone in his hand directing something going on with the stage. "One, two, three. Step to the right. Wave. Step to the left. Wave. And don't forget to smile, ladies. And bow at the end of the runway. Make your Southern mamas proud."

"My Southern Mama has been dead for years." I heard a familiar voice followed up by some snickers. Just as I walked in view of the tent, Viola White bent down to the ground in a curtsey. The red feather boa around her neck shed small little feathers as she struggled to get back up.

"I'm not going to be able to get back up and throw kisses to all my loyal supporters." She finally got up and stuck her hand on her hip. She wore a bright yellow turban on the top of her head that perfectly matched the color of her wrap that was loosely draped around her shoulders. Barely sticking out from underneath the layers of feather boa was a gold necklace with balls the size of baseballs that had to've been hurting her neck. It made my neck hurt just looking at it.

"Get off the stage, Viola! Let the Snow Queen have her rehearsal." Mama stepped up the side stairs, stage right. "One, two, three, one, two, three," she repeated like a little girl that was in dance class as her legs glided like she was ice skating.

It was very odd and looked very strange. I stood behind a pole that'd been wrapped with garland and so many Christmas ornaments that no one was going to see me.

"Wave and bow." She abruptly stopped. "Is it wave and bow or bow and wave?" Mama put her hand over her eyes so she could shield them from the lights that were shining on the stage.

"It's step to the left and wave, then step to the right." The man showed Mama.

"I know. You don't have to show me. I was a debutant." She sucked in a deep breath and stuck out her chest. "Move to the right. Wave," she whispered and did that darn hand thing she'd been doing.

"Wait!" The man yelled. "What is this?" The man snarled and did the strange wave. "This is not appropriate."

"It's the Queen's wave and I'm going to do whatever I want." Mama was getting upset.

I closed my eyes and took a gulp in hopes I wasn't going to have to step in because this man clearly had no idea who Vivian Lowry was and she by no means had any problem letting him know.

"I'm not sure," The man started to say before I stepped out from behind the pole.

"Good early afternoon," I smiled at him. "Hello, Mama." I waved. "You're looking mighty good up there."

"Shep, that's my daughter, Kendrick Lowry. Sheriff Lowry of Cottonwood." Mama hated the fact I was sheriff but was more than happy to use the title when she felt like it was going to get her something.

"I just stopped by to make sure everything was okay out here," I said.

"We are fine. I was just showing Shep my wave like the Queen." She continued to walk the front of the stage. "Elbow, wrist, elbow, wrist and then the wave."

"She's got it down pat doesn't she?" I asked Shep. What kind of name was Shep? "She's been practicing a long time."

By the look of the light bulb going off in his head, I could see he knew that I was just telling him that it was better to let her go than to correct her.

"I'm sure you've got your hands full with all these women." I turned my attention to him while Mama continued to do her ice skating moves and weird waves.

"Only with your Mama and Viola White. Those two might have a fist fight." He shrugged. "I'm not sure I'd stop it either. I've never seen two women their ages wanting so badly to be crowned queen."

"I'm taking it that you aren't from here or the South?" I asked.

"Neither, honey." His nose snarled. "I'm doing this as a favor for the county pageant officials. Unfortunately, they decided to send me to nowhere Kentucky."

TANGLED UP IN TINSEL 145

"I'm sure you'll find our little slice of nowhere to be quite charming if you'll let it. How long are you in town for?" I asked and noticed Jolee's food truck pulling into the fairgrounds.

"Only until after the pageant. I'm leaving that night on a red-eye back to California so I can be home with my loved ones for Christmas."

"That's nice. Well, if you do need anything, you give me a holler." I pulled a business card from my back pocket since I was in street clothes.

"Holler?" He asked sarcastically. "As in a yee-haw kinda Kentucky thing?"

"Just a word of advice, Shep," I leaned in real close and said real stern, "Around here, we take our little hillbilly world to heart."

He drew back as if I offended him.

"You are referring to us as hillbillies," I made no room for him to correct me. "And by no means take our accents as ignorance. We are very kind and smart people. If you just stay focused on why you are here and maybe take whatever stick is stuck up your you-know-what, you might find that you'll enjoy our little town here in Kentucky."

At this point, I'd had my fill of Mr. Shep and I would let him deal with the arguing that Mama and Viola seemed to be involved in on stage left as I dismissed myself and made my way back to the far end of the fairground where I could see rows of trees all tied up to different tomato stakes. Above the trees there were strung twinkling Christmas lights that outlined the entire tree lot.

On the side of the lot, I could see Darnell's truck pulled up with the lift gate down. There were a few boys hauling freshly cut trees out of the back of it. Kenneth Chalk, the football coach, had his whistle in his mouth and was directing the boys where to go with the firs.

"You're like a drill sergeant," I joked when Coach came to greet me after he saw me walking up.

"Gotta be strict with these young men or they jump out of line real quick." He put his hand out for me to shake. "Sheriff, how are you?" A knit stocking hat covered up his bald head.

"You know. Same old, same old." I tucked my hands in the pocket of my jacket. "It could be a little warmer though."

"Oh no," he shook his head. "Perfect for a white Christmas."

"You and I both know that weather around here changes with the wind." I hated to see everyone get their hopes up about this big snow storm that never was going to happen.

"Even so, you better pick you out a nice tree to look at over the next week or so because if we do get that big snow storm, you won't be leaving your house for days." His brows furrowed. "I guess you might somehow since you're the sheriff and could get some calls."

"I'm not going to need a big tree this year. I'm actually going to take a little vacation." I watched the boys to see if I recognized them from the dance.

"Vacation? At Christmas?" He acted as if it was the strangest thing he'd ever heard. "I thought your Mama was in the running for Snow Queen."

"I'm going to go meet Finn's family in Chicago. I guess I'm going to miss the big crowning." The girl I'd seen arguing with Manuel had walked up to one of the boys hauling trees out of Coach's truck. It wasn't polite to walk away from Coach, so I watched her every move.

"That'll break your mama's heart. That's none of my business. But she'll make it everyone's business." A hint of a smile made the corner of his lip turn up.

"I'm actually here to see you." I watched the girl hastily talking to the boy. He jerked his arm away from her and she stormed off into the tree lot, leaving him to do his job. "I wanted to know if you knew of anything strange with one of your old and current players."

"You're referring to the Libertys." He rolled his eyes. "At least Sean Graves isn't here this year to ruin our fundraiser. Is this about the Graves girl?" He asked. "I sure hated to hear that she was found in the river. Do you think an animal ran out in front of her?"

"I'm not sure, but I'd love to get your take on the Liberty home situation," I said.

"You asking about Manuel turning down his college opportunity?" He asked, and I nodded. "Well, if he were my boy, I'd made him take it, but his mam doesn't have no control over those boys."

"What do you mean?" I asked.

"Them two boys of hers run around all night. Take Jonathon for instance. He's a good player and he might be better than Manuel, but he can't keep up with his grades or keep his head on straight. I went to Juanita and told her but she's so distraught over Manuel and the Graves girl, she didn't want to discuss either of her other two boys." He leaned in. "Over the past couple of days, I've never seen the woman so happy. She's been here volunteering and singing. She don't care one bit that her boy is trying to mend a broken heart over his girlfriend's death. Beats me." He shrugged.

"Your Mama makes the best fruit cakes." He pointed to his truck. Mama must've been up to her tricks of giving out her famous sweets for a vote for Snow Queen. "She brought me one this morning. Good woman your Mama is. Anyways, for your sake, I hope you get out of here in time for your vacation. You sure do deserve it." His eyes softened. "Now what about that sheriff's department donation this year?"

During the year, the sheriff's department, the three of us (Me, Finn and Betty), always put our spare change in a big ole glass whiskey jar that sat on the ground. At the end of each year we liked to pick a charity to donate the saved money to, and generally we had around five hundred dollars which wasn't bad for some change.

"You know, I need to check with Betty Murphy on that."

He dragged his stocking cap off his head and rubbed it.

"Alright. You stop on down to the department and pick up your annual donation," I told him and took my hands out of my pocket.

I rubbed them vigorously. I swore the air was even ten degrees colder since I'd been standing here.

"Is that the Palmer girl over there with Beka Durst?" I questioned the coach since I knew he knew all the kids in school while I took my phone out of my back pocket and quickly texted Betty to write a check out to Cottonwood High School for our annual donation.

"Yeah. She came back this year to help with the lot while home from college. She's a sweet girl." He pinched his lips. "I'm not sure what happened, but she and the Graves girl used to be real close."

"I'd heard that. It was great talking with you. Good luck." I gestured to the trees. "I'm gonna pick me out one before I get out of here."

The carolers had moved around while I'd been shooting the breeze with Coach. At least during our conversation, I'd found out that Juanita had almost completely taken over as the head volunteer over the past couple of days.

I watched Mama as she walked over to the food truck, this time with a big sash diagonal across her body that read "Snow Princess" in gold glitter.

I hurried inside of the trees before Mama could see me because if she did get a minute to corner me, she'd asked all about the Graves and I wasn't prepared to make a statement just yet.

The young girl I wanted to talk to was out sitting at the card table with Beka. A metal money box that I'd seen at many of the gates of the Cottonwood High School home football games was on top of the table.

"Hi, Beka," I greeted her. "How's your Mama doing?"

"She's fine," she answered. Her hair was pulled up in a high ponytail like the other little cheerleaders running around. "She's busy running the tow company while the Graves take off a few days. You know, for the memorial and all." She looked at Rachel and frowned.

"Are you going to the memorial?" Rachel asked Beka.

"If mom gets the work done. She's got to log the mileage on the tows and keep them filled with gas, which takes up a lot of time."

Mileage? Her word circled my brain when it flicked my gut.

"You're thinking now." Poppa ghosted next to a small fir tree that stood up next to the girl's table. "This is perfect for your house this year. Plus, I know mileage could tell if one of the Graves's tow trucks was used the night of Leighann's murder." Poppa's thoughts were all over the place.

He took the words right out of my mouth, on both, and I tucked that thought in the back of my head.

"She's doing a good thing." I confirmed. I turned my eyes upon the girl with her. "Are you Rachel Palmer?" I asked the girl.

"Yes." She looked at Beka and they both shrugged at each other.

"I'm Sheriff Lowry and I wanted to know if I could talk to you about Leighann Graves." Both girls' eyes grew big.

"Sure." She and Beka could pass as twins. Both had on the varsity letter jacket that had "cheerleader" sewn on the back. "I'll be right back."

I couldn't help but notice Beka grab her phone and start texting. I was sure she was letting all the kids in high school know I was going to talk to Rachel.

They even had on the same eye shadow, lipstick and hair pulled back as tight as bark on a tree in a high ponytail.

"Would you like a hot chocolate?" I asked after we walked out of the tree lot and I noticed Mama was no long at the food truck. One of Jolee Fischer's homemade fudgy hot chocolates with mini-marshmallows sounded really good about right now.

"I'd love one if you're paying because I have no cash whatsoever. If I didn't have to work this stupid tree lot for the team, I'd be home in my warm bed. Poor college kid." Rachel Palmer was no different than Leighann Graves. No wonder they were friends.

"I thought you were volunteering?" I asked.

"I am, but Coach usually gives out a little gift card at the end. I sure could use it," she said.

"Sheriff," Jolee's eyes skimmed over me and focused on the girl. "Hi, Rachel. I'm sorry to hear about Leighann."

"Yeah, me too," The girl replied. "I'll have a hot chocolate on her."

"Okay." Jolee's eyes got big and when she directed her attention to me, I nodded. "Two?"

"Two and extra marshmallows." I held my fingers in the air. "Why don't we go sit under the shelter where they are holding the Snow Queen pageant?"

Rachel shrugged.

"Do you mind bringing us the drinks?" I asked Jolee.

"Nope. It'll be a second. My fudge is in the oven." She looked behind me. "Can I help you?" she asked the next person in line behind me and Rachel.

We headed over to the shelter where there were picnic tables in the back. The front was already filled with folding chairs in anticipation of the tree lighting.

"There's the tree." Rachel pointed to the truck hauling a hitched trailer with a big pine tree on it. "We also get to decorate it."

"The team?" I asked, and we sat down on the very far right picnic table closest to the food truck.

"Yeah. Leighann loved doing that when we were cheerleaders." She gave a slight grin as if she was having the memory play in her head. Her arms propped up on the table.

"I saw the two of you arguing at the Hunt Club dance." She stared at me with blank eyes as I talked. "Can you tell me about it?"

"I'm so upset that she's dead, but she's the one who changed everything." Rachel sat back and put her hands in the letter jacket front pockets.

"How so?" I asked.

"She and I were going to go to Bluegrass College together last year. We had it all planned out. The sorority we were going to join. The dorm where we were going to live. Matching bedding and all the fun monogramed stuff. Then," she rolled her eyes, "Manuel Liberty got buff and decided he could be the football star and steal her heart." Her words held a real bitter tone.

"Is that a problem?" I asked.

"It is when my boyfriend was the head football star and supposed to get a full scholarship to Bluegrass College. Then Bluegrass College decided to look at Manuel instead. That became a real problem. Neither of our boyfriends could stand the other. It didn't help that Manuel is a bit of a bully." She rambled on and stopped when Jolee walked over with the steaming cups of hot chocolate.

"Here you go." She sat down a baggie full of marshmallows. "Extra goodness."

"Thanks," I said and handed Rachel the bag first. Jolee walked back to her truck. "What does this have to do with you and Leighann?"

"She decided that she wanted to go with Manuel since she started dating him." Slowly she stirred the hot chocolate with the wooden stir and blew on the steamy goodiness.

"Both decided not to go to college. Why?" I asked about the new name she threw in.

"Whatever Manuel wanted, Leighann wanted too." She said it in that duh kind of way that made me thank god I wasn't a teenager. She pulled out her phone. "How long is this little talk of ours going to take? Beka needs me."

"You and Beka close?" I asked.

"We're friends. I didn't hang with her much in high school since she's a year younger." She threw some more marshmallows in the cup.

"It looks like there's a lot of boys that can help her manage."

I wanted to ask her some more questions. "Can you tell me what you and Leighann were arguing about at the dance?"

"Last year when she worked up the nerve to tell her parents, who by the way are head cases," she put her hands in the air to get her point across, "that she wasn't going to college. She was going to take a gap year. That's when I realized she was leaving me high and dry to go to Bluegrass by myself. It was too late to get a roommate at that point, so I had to go with an unknown. The worst."

"What was the fight about the other night?" I couldn't understand how she could lose me so fast. I'd ask her a question and she'd circle it back to nothing I needed to know.

"I'm trying to forget about that. Especially since it was the last time I'd talked to her," Rachel's voice cracked. "I ran into Leighann in the bathroom and when I ignored her, she got up in my business. I told her I had nothing to say to her since she ruined our plans. When I left the bathroom and saw her and Manuel making out by the punch bowl, I about barfed." Her head was moving back and forth as she told the story as if she were right back in the situation. "I marched right back up to her and told her that I actually wanted to thank her for dumping me because I'd met a bunch of new friends and she didn't have any because Manuel made sure she didn't." She shrugged and pressed her lips together, which evidently had a direct line to quirk her right brow, because she did this a lot when she talked. "I regret it."

"You had no way of knowing that she was going to pass away." I wanted to offer some sort of comfort, though I still had more questions. "He made her stop having friends?" I asked to clarify my thoughts. Before now, I thought Leighann had chosen to dump her friends.

"He's a loser. After they started dating, she'd cancel our plans because Manuel didn't want her to go or didn't think she should do whatever it was we were going to do. I can't believe she wasted what time on earth she had with him. I can't even believe I was friends with her. When friends make promises, they keep them." She brought her hand up to her head to push back a stray piece of hair that'd fallen out of the ponytail, exposing a tattoo heart on the fatty part of her thumb. Just like the one Leighann had.

"Tell me about your tattoo." I pointed to her hand.

"It was a big mistake I'd made with Leighann. Now," she spoke softly and ran her finger over it. "I will treasure it because we got it when we were the best of friends and before all this happened." She gulped. "'Friends forever tattoos' was what we called them." She rubbed the tattoo like she was trying to rub it away. "After she ended our friendship, I wanted to get it removed. Actually," She folded her hands between her knees, "Manuel is the one who ended our friendship."

"Clearly, you're still very hurt by it." I watched her body language as she struggled with being upset and trying to hide it.

"How do you think you'd feel after you made all these plans and suddenly they were changed?" She asked. "While I was at school, I'd forgotten all about her. Now that I'd seen her and now that she's dead, it's all come back." She stood up. "I'm super sad she's dead because I'll never ever get to make it right with her. I'm not sure I can live with that."

"After your fight at the Christmas Cantata, where did you go?" I asked.

"That's a whole nuther thing. I went home." Her country accent deepened. "If I'd known my parents made me have a curfew when I came home after having freedom while away at college, I might not've come home for Christmas."

"What time is your curfew?" I asked.

"Midnight," she replied with a sarcastic tone. "Ridiculous. Like I'm some baby. Even Beka's curfew is later and she's still in high school."

"Before you go, how is your roommate in college now?" I asked.

"Great." She frowned. "I'm not sure I'd have so many new friends if Leighann had gone with me. She's a one-friend person and with my new roommate, we joined a sorority and we've met all sorts of people not from around here."

"I'm glad you're enjoying it. Bye, Rachel." I waved, knowing in my heart that she didn't kill Leighann even though I knew I'd be able to confirm where she was by tracking her phone that never left her hand and talking with her parents.

The tree fit the perfect length of the roof of the Wagoneer. Not too tall and not too short. Perfect for a little Christmas cheer while I was here. It was tied down nicely by Jonathon Liberty and Beka Durst.

"Thanks." I gave them both a couple of ones for a tip. "It's not much, but it's something."

"Man, every little bit helps with college." Jonathon seemed grateful and stuck it in his pocket.

"I've been saving up for some new lipstick for my Mama for Christmas. This helps." Beka stuck it in her pocket and walked away.

"Jonathan, I wanted to talk to you," I said.

"Yeah. My mom told me you were going to question me about when we went all loaded up on old man Graves. We didn't have any bullets." He tried not to grin as he told the story. "That man is a jerk. I swear it was the guns that made him change his mind about my bro and Leighann."

"How so?" I asked, restraining from reprimanding him.

"That's the same week that Leighann told them she wasn't going to college and she and Manuel had decided to stay in Cottonwood." His eyes slid over to his mama's. She was standing with a customer but looking at us. "Mom was so mad though."

Jonathon gnawed on the side of his cheek as though he was trying to hold back something.

"Jonathan." I reached out and touched his arm to bring him back to the present. "If there's something you need to tell me, it's safe with me."

"My mom will kill me, but I know that you think she's a suspect. Far from it." He looked down at his feet and pushed around some dirt with the toe of his boot. "Truth is, my mom has Crohn's and she's not getting better. She only wanted what's best for us. Since Manuel is the oldest, he took it upon himself not to go to college and work, so he can provide."

He bit back the emotions I could see swelling up inside of him.

"Mom was mad and blamed Leighann for it. But in reality, it's her sickness that kept him here," his voice cracked.

One after the other, little town secrets were coming to light. First, Sean Graves being an abuser and now Juanita Liberty's illness. Now I wasn't so sure she didn't kill Leighann.

"Where were you the night of Leighann's murder?" I asked him.

"At home. Mom had a little set back that day. I had to take care of the kids while Manuel went to meet Leighann at the dance. When he got home around eleven, he said I could go on out, but I was slap worn out. Mom had finally fallen asleep." He shoved his hands in his pocket. "I'm no cop or nothing, but I know Leighann didn't get along with Sean at all."

"Thanks. I might stop by and talk to your other brothers." I gave him a little warning just in case I wanted to check out all the stories. "And another thing, your brother looks up to you and gun slinging is no way to teach him a lesson."

"That's what my mom said. She was fit to be tied after Sean Graves called her. All the business about 'we are better than them' and all that." He looked over at his mom. "She's a good woman. She's done the best she could with us unruly boys. Leighann was strong like Mom, but Mom was upset about Manuel's decision and I think it was easier for her to blame Leighann and not herself. She didn't want the world to know she was sick. Just her and Dr. Shively."

"If there's anything you boys need, or even your mama, you can always call me." I wanted him to know that I was there to help in any way.

He simply nodded and walked away.

Chapter Thirteen

"She's got Crohn's?" Finn hung the silver tinsel around the back side of the tree and I took it from him to carry it around to the front, then back again. "That doesn't make her innocent."

"I think that if she's in pain and in bed like Jonathon said, then she couldn't physically have taken all the steps and moved Leighann around like a rag doll."

"I bet deep down she knew that Manuel stayed because of her." Finn made a good point.

We did the tinsel wrap around the small tree until there was none left.

"Why didn't Leighann tell her parents that's why he stayed?" I asked.

"True. Maybe they'd been more sympathetic to the situation." Finn shrugged.

"I also talked to Rachel Palmer, Leighann's best friend. She claimed she had a curfew and was at home that night, but I'd talked to her mom before I talked to her. She too confirmed Rachel was home."

"What was their deal the other night?" He asked and walked out from behind the tree.

"It seemed all like immature teenage angst junk that just

escalated. Rachel and Leighann were best friends. When Leighann and Manuel started dating, it appeared the friendship started to go south. Leighann stopped hanging around her friends." I opened the ornament box and started to hang the ornaments on the tree. "Then Leighann had skipped out on them going away to college together and even rooming together. Rachel still harbors bad feelings of betrayal."

"Oh no." Finn bent down and looked over the ornaments. "Are you and your friends hanging out less because of us?"

"Don't be ridiculous." I pushed him on the ground and snuggled up to him while we looked at all the colored lights we'd put on the tree first.

Duke bounced around us. He gave a few woofs thinking we were playing with him when I was trying to break the sudden mood from happily putting up a Christmas tree to talking about the murder.

"My Poppa used to put his tree in this same spot." I rested on my elbow and hip. "He would love it. All these colored lights."

"It's beautiful, just like you." Finn reached over and tucked a strand of hair behind my ear.

"You aren't even looking at the tree," I said.

"I'm looking at you. Tell me something else about your Christmas past." His encouraging me only opened up the flood gates.

"Well, when I as a little girl and we did get all this snow every year, he would get a real sled and some of his friends' horses to pull us in sleigh rides." The memories were so vivid in my head, just like it was yesterday. "He'd have hot chocolate on the sled and warm quilt blankets. He'd have them take us down to the courthouse lawn where they had the big Christmas tree.

This was way before the fairgrounds had the tree lighting event."

"That was one time only?" Finn asked and snuggled up close behind me, resting his chin in-between my ear and shoulder.

"It was a couple of times but then the weather started to get warmer and warmer, so we would just drive down to the tree lighting." I tried to swallow the big lump in my throat because talking about it made me realize that this was the first year that I'd not been here when they did light up the tree. "Just like this year with me going with you. Things change."

"Are you trying to convince me that you're not going to miss out on the tradition or convince yourself that it's going to be okay?" He asked. "Because if you aren't okay with it, I don't mind going to Chicago by myself. You can meet my parents anytime."

"No." I jiggled my body around to face him. "Don't be ridiculous. This just can't be a take and no give relationship." Though I suddenly wanted to burst into tears. I had to get up and stop talking about it. "And if I don't want my friends to dump me, then I've got to get to Euchre."

"I'll clean up here, feed Duke and head on home." He reached up and extended his hand for me to help him up, only his real ploy was to tug me down into his arms for some more snuggles before I really had to go.

This week's Euchre night was at Tibbie Bells's house. We had decided she had the best house out of all of us and she didn't have a boyfriend, children or pets to worry with.

Tibbie lived right off Main Street on what we referred to as the Town Branch. There was a small water brook, or branch, that ran the length of the street. Every house had a small concrete bridge that gapped the street to the driveway. The houses were old like most of the houses in Cottonwood and so were the bridges. Most of the time the small creek was dried up and not much water flowed these days, but it was still some history and part of my childhood that made Cottonwood the cozy, Southern town all of us loved.

The room on the left was where Tibbie had all the tables for the Sweet Adelines to put their food. I'd like to say it was the best part of the night, but it wasn't. The best part was the hissy fits and fights that the Euchre tournament brought out in everyone. This was especially good since there'd be a lot of talk about Leighann's death. This was when Poppa always told me to keep my ear to the ground because somewhere in all that gossip there was some truth.

Still, I grabbed a plate at the end of one table and perused all the finger foods that I'd call my supper.

"Good gracious, didn't I see you in that outfit today?" Betty asked as she slid up to the right side of me.

"What was all this nonsense I heard down at the jewelry store that you were using Sterling as a deputy?" Viola White eyeballed me as she came up on the left of me. "Now, I might be old and halfway senile, but I do know that my good earned tax dollars do not pay for Sterling."

"You got two things right," Mama said and snuck up behind me. "You are old and senile."

"Oh shut up, Viv. You ain't too far behind and with zero grandchildren I might add." Viola's eye drew up and down me. "If you don't get that baby factory kicked in gear, you'll have to shut down production."

"My production is just fine, thank you. Ain't that right, Camille?" I asked Camille Shively, the only doctor in Cottonwood when she walked into the room.

"I'm pleading the fifth. I knew not to come tonight. Nothing ever goes well at these events." Camille picked up a meatball and popped it into her mouth. "Mmmm, good."

"It's a shame about that Graves girl." Myrna Savage walked in with a big container of poinsettias. "That's for you, honey. Merry Christmas," she said to Tibbie and handed them to her.

"Why thank you. They are lovely." Tibbie took a few cheery steps across the room and replaced the Dixon Foodtown flowers with the poinsettias, though I didn't know why she just didn't put them somewhere else since Myrna Savage also supplied the grocer with fresh flowers from her greenhouse.

"Anyways, about that Graves girl." Myrna sashayed though the crowd of beady little eyes that suddenly focused on me. "You know anything yet?"

"Now, now, Myrna," I wagged a finger. "You know I can't give out any official details."

I moved on down the line and filled my plate with Christmas bark, fancy holiday cookies and a couple of slices of pie, skipping the hanky-panky and any sort of meat dish that might be healthier than the sweet treats I'd opted for.

"The Christmas Cantata turned out nice." I saddled up to Tibbie in the other room where she was finishing setting up the four-person-each card tables where we'd start our Euchre games. "You did another fine job."

"Thanks." Her hazel eyes had a twinkle in them. "I really enjoy my job," she said and referred to her event planning occupation. Her long brown hair was normally parted down the middle, but tonight she wore it in a deep side part and fishtail braid down the side of her head. "Are you all ready for your big trip?"

"I am. That doesn't mean I won't miss y'all." I reached over and squeezed her arm.

I had to throw it in there since I was going to miss our annual movie night that Jolee had already scolded me for, but I certainly didn't want me and my friends to end up like Leighann and Rachel. Though I'd hoped we were much wiser since we were older.

"This is exciting though." Her shoulders rose up with excitement. "You're going to go to Chicago for the first time and it's going to be so romantic. What if the snowstorm hits there instead and when you wake up on Christmas, it'll be a white one just like the movie."

"If it is, I sure don't see Finn singing 'Snow'." I laughed.

"You could sing 'White Christmas'." She laughed. "But knowing Finn, I don't think so."

"Are you going to Leighann's memorial tomorrow afternoon?" Tibbie asked.

"Tomorrow?" I halted with shock.

Neither myself nor Max had cleared Leighann's body to be handed over to the family.

"By the way you are acting, I'd take it as a no." She peered at me. "You seem a little shocked."

"I'd not heard about it and since I've not cleared her body to the family, it's a bit shocking." I wondered what'd transpired.

"It's a memorial. They said they weren't having a body. The church phone line is abuzz with food for it." Tibbie nodded. "I have no idea how I got in charge of the phone line, but now I wished I'd turned it down. But you know if I'd done that, my mom would've died of embarrassment." She nudged me. "You know we good Southern daughters always make our mamas proud." She winked.

The phone line was technically a gossip hot line. In between there was some sort of organization on who was bringing what to a funeral or memorial or even the birth of a baby.

"They are going to bury her in a private funeral later." Tibbie's brow rose as her chin lifted up and then down.

"Very interesting," I muttered and walked into the other room to join the other card players.

The room had started to fill with the girls and they were already taking their seats with their partners. Jolee and I had to play Mama and Viola White, which was going to be interesting to say the least since they had this little competition thing going with Snow Queen. Sometimes it drove me nuts how competitive Mama really was.

Camille Shively had walked into the room and while Tibbie continued to set multiple card decks down along with pens and paper, I took the moment to see exactly what the good doctor knew.

"Kenni, you know that I can't tell you what's in a patient's file." She always used the client privilege law on me.

"I just want to know how long Sean Graves has been on Ambien. And what stage of Crohn's disease Juanita Liberty is in. That's all. Don't make me go to a judge and get a subpoena when you can just tell me." It was a little dance she and I did that made things so interesting between us.

It wasn't like Camille and I were best friends or even good friends when we were growing up. She was the young pretty girl with beautiful black hair that only movie stars could afford, only hers was real and not from a bottle down at Tiny Tina's. She had the perfect skin and black eyes. She was like a real-life Snow White.

She was real smart too. She'd decided to become a doctor and move back to Cottonwood because our doctor at the time was knocking on death's door and she knew eventually she'd have the market, kinda like Max Bogus in the death industry.

"Why don't you stop by my office tomorrow and bring me the filled-out paper work that you'd submit to the judge. It's a lot more private there." She twisted her head around. "Everyone will suddenly know everything if we talk here."

"I'll be by around lunch," I told her because I had to go talk to Angela Durst, the Graves' secretary.

The games got underway and Mama was the dealer.

"Cut the cards?" She asked, holding the deck out. I knocked on it to pass. The knocking was an enduring Euchre term.

"I'm not cutting my luck. I need all the luck I can get," I said.

"Speaking of luck, how unlucky was it that poor Leighann got luck of the draw with Sean?" Viola snarled over the cards. "I'd like to beat that man."

"You and the rest of Cottonwood," Mama nodded and dealt two cards to everyone and then three to finish out, so we could start the hand. "I remember when they signed the adoption papers."

"Adoption papers?" My head jerked up.

"Don't you know?" Mama asked and all of us passed on the trump card she'd flipped over on the throwaway deck. All of us passed again before she called hearts as trump. "I'll go it alone," she proclaimed and shoved the throwaway deck over to Viola.

"I hope you play this hand better than you're playing your cards at the pageant," Viola whispered under her voice. "But I trust my partner."

Mama eyed Viola before she slid her gaze to the cards fanned in her hands. She led with the Jack of Hearts as she drew out the hearts in mine and Jolee's hands.

"I don't know what, Mama? Concentrate," I encouraged her.

"I am concentrating," she snipped back.

"I mean on the story." My last nerve was tickling my anger that I felt welling up in me. "Don't I know what?" I asked again.

"Leighann isn't Sean's daughter. He adopted her when he and Jilly got married. She was just a tiny tot and cute as a button," Mama dragged off topic.

Jolee and I threw our cards in the middle when we realized that Mama was going to take every card trick with her hearts and win four points.

"You're telling me that Sean Graves isn't Leighann Graves biological father?" I sat there dumbfounded.

"That's probably why he felt like it was okay to be mean to the girl," Viola said with a stern-faced expression.

I didn't know how I made it through the rest of the Euchre tournament. We'd even turned out the nightly winner. With this new information that'd come to light about Leighann being adopted, it put the desperate father, Sean Graves, in a completely different light.

Chapter Fourteen

"How did you not know about this and live here all your life?" Finn asked over a cup of steaming coffee as both of us stared across the diner table at each other the next morning.

"I was a kid myself when this happened." I really had tried to think back to when I was a kid to remember. "I would've been around twelve years old when that happened. I was riding around with Poppa and playing records, not wondering what was going on with people I went to church with. It wasn't like they just showed up in Cottonwood one day. They both lived here."

"Who is the dad?" Finn asked.

"I have no idea. I even asked around at Euchre and Mama said that was one of the biggest mysteries in Cottonwood." I held the cup of coffee up to my lips and took a sip. "Now that I think back in the investigation since her death, he's never called Leighann his daughter."

"What about before she was killed and all those times he'd called about Manuel?" He eased back and let Ben put a biscuits and gravy plate down in front of him and one in front of me.

"Are you talking about the Graves?" Ben sat down in the empty seat next to me. "I was going to tell you that something strange happened the week before Leighann died."

"What?" I asked. Then I put my hand up. "Is this on record?"

"Sure." He nodded.

"What happened?" I asked and pinched off a piece of my biscuit, giving it to Duke.

"That local slimeball lawyer, Wally Lamb, was in here with Jilly Graves. They were sitting right over there in that corner table away from everyone." He pointed to the far corner opposite us next to the kitchen. "I offered them a table up front since the kitchen can be loud."

"They didn't want anyone to hear them." Poppa ghosted in the seat next to Finn. My lashes lowered, and I glared at him. "Oh, ding, ding." He winked.

"Then she left and Leighann came in." Ben looked over his shoulder when another early customer came through the door. "I'll be right with you." They made eye contact. The customer walked up to the counter. He continued, "Leighann was crying saying that her mom deserved better and hoped that her mom could get half of the business. That's when I heard something about divorce. Leighann really brought on the tears after Manuel and Juanita came in."

"Divorce?" Finn, me and Poppa all asked at the same time.

"Now, I don't know for sure, but Jolee told me that Sean was an abuser and it dawned on me what'd taken place right over there and it's something I just can't swallow without reporting it." Ben stood up and topped off our coffee mugs before he left to go take care of the other customers.

"The kitchen was covering up their voices so no one could hear them." I was getting really good at repeating Poppa and his observations.

"Right." Finn snapped his fingers. "Maybe she was telling him something about the abuse and trying to stop it."

"Maybe Sean didn't know that she was thinking about divorce and Leighann confronted him about it, and out of anger—resentment maybe—took out Leighann and planned to do away with Jilly. But Jilly called us about Leighann's disappearance before he could hurt her." It was a far-fetched idea and plan, but it gave us more clues to go on. Not to mention made Sean Graves more of a suspect.

"Every other time they've called about Leighann with Manuel, wasn't it Sean that did the calling not Jilly?" Finn asked.

"Yes. This time it was her. But we need to double check." I pointed to our plates. "We better eat so it doesn't get cold and we can get out of here."

For the next ten minutes, there might've been silence between us but I could tell that his mind was going as fast as mine on conspiracies and why Sean Graves would kill Leighann.

Before we even realized, we were down the street at the department looking up old files and records from when Sean Graves had called the department about Manuel. Duke had climbed in his bed and curled into a tight ball. He liked cold weather but not the bitter and depressing cold that'd hung over the entire town of Cottonwood.

"There are fifteen times in the past two years." I kept my finger on the last one. "The last time he'd called was right before she'd turned eighteen."

"Then it appeared that he'd just washed his hands of her." Finn brushed his hands together. "No longer responsible for her."

"That's why he made it easier to toss her out of the house,"

Scott spoke up from the makeshift desk he'd made near the fax machine.

"That's not entirely true." I glanced up at the clock. It was nearing eight a.m. "I'm going to go see Angela Durst, the secretary of Graves Towing. I'd heard she'd taken in Leighann when Sean kicked her out."

"This is all very interesting." Scott had a perplexed look on his face.

"Oh my God," I gasped. My eyes shot over to Poppa. "Sean did say that he went to Chimney Rock that night to see if Leighann and Manuel were there."

"Covering his tracks." Poppa's eyes lowered. "If I was alive, I'd give him a good ole one-two." Poppa jabbed the air with his best boxing moves.

The door opened, and Betty walked in.

"Weee-doggy." She gave a shimmy-shake. "I wish that storm would blow in and get it over with. I'm so tired of hearing the news and radio about it. It's cold as a gravestone out there."

We all snickered, and she looked up.

"What? What are y'all staring at? Did something happen?" She dragged her pocket book from her elbow and sat it down on her desk before she peeled off her coat and flung it on the back of her chair.

"Betty," I stood up and patted my leg. "Get the cell ready. We might have a customer by the end of the day."

"Really?" She gasped in delight.

It wasn't every day, heck wasn't every week that we got to use the only cell in the room and I could feel it. I was getting close to solving this murder.

"Finn, do you mind checking up on the report of Leighann's phone records? Scott, can you check with the forensics on the side panel to make sure it was a match?" I asked and gathered my bag and patted my leg for Duke to come. "I've got to go get some answers from the eyes and ears of Graves Towing: Angela Durst."

"Don't forget about what you told me about Camille Shively," Finn reminded me how I'd told him over coffee that Camille told me to bring the subpoenaed paperwork and she'd take a look at it and possibly give me what I needed without actually going through a judge.

The Wagoneer took much longer to heat up than normal. I kept sliding the old knob to the right to see if it'd go any further.

"It's an old Jeep. You've got to be tender and gentle with her." Poppa patted the dashboard, just like he used to when I was a kid. "It's not a modern-day fancy car."

"Now that we are alone." I stopped the Jeep at the stop light and zipped up my coat. "What is your take on the new light of things?"

"I think that Sean looks very suspicious. I'm not sure what killing Leighann would do for him." Poppa brought in the logical side of things. "Did she have something on him other than he hated Manuel? After this divorce or whatever Ben had witnessed, was there going to be some sort of information? Why would he drug her first and not her mama? That's not logical at all."

"I'm not sure, but you can bet your bottom dollar we are going to find out," I said in a hushed whisper on our way back out to Graves Towing.

"The sky sure looks grey." Poppa looked out window. "Do you remember when it snowed a lot when you were a kid and I'd gotten that sled?"

"Best memory of winter I've got." I blinked back a tear and

looked over at him, but he'd ghosted away.

Poppa was never one for sentimental feelings. He was a tough old geezer and that's what made him a great sheriff. There was a legacy I had to hold up to and I prayed I was doing so, even in the midst of a murder.

The tow company sign was flashing on and a little bit in me wished Sean had closed the company, but a business was a business.

"Hi-do, Kenni," Angela Durst greeted me from her desk. "If you're here to see Jilly or Sean, they are gone to the funeral home. They are having a quick memorial tonight and tomorrow is going to be the funeral without the body since...well, you know the circumstances."

Max wasn't releasing Leighann's body until all the facts were presented for a final report and I'd gotten it. We didn't want to just turn the body over and maybe miss something. It was a little early for the Graves to have decided to do something. It'd only been a couple of days.

"No. I came here to see you." I took a couple of steps closer to her desk. "I know you practically run the place."

"I wouldn't say that." She blushed. "But you're right. I'm not sure what I can do for you though. Does this have to do with Leighann?"

"I'd heard that you took Leighann in when Sean kicked her out. Is that right?" I asked.

"Let's just say that now I wished I'd done more." Tears lined her lids. "She was such a sweet girl. She was young and in love."

"Can you tell me about your relationship with her? A confidant? A friend?" I asked. "Beka her friend?"

"I guess you could say that she and Beka were friends. I

mean," she shrugged, "Beka grew up here next to me when I worked and she and Leighann played a lot together. She's the one who told me that she'd overheard Sean kick Leighann out."

"What did she overhear?" I asked.

"She can tell you herself." Angela pushed her chair back from her desk and got up. "She's in the back filing some paperwork."

While she headed down the hall to get Beka, I noticed the shelving behind her desk. They were black binders that were labeled on the spine with dates. I walked over and dragged my finger down them, pulling the latest one out. When I flipped it open, it was a mileage spreadsheet with the vin number of the tow truck and the date.

"Hi, Beka." I replaced the binder when I heard them walk back in. "I guess I should've asked you at the tree lot about your relationship with Leighann."

She looked at her mom with a confused and scared look on her face.

"It's okay. She's going to figure out who did this to Leighann. You need to tell her about what Leighann told you about Sean." Her mom encouraged her. "And what you overheard."

"I'm accusing no one of hurting her." Beka wanted to clarify with me.

"I'm not saying you are. I'm just trying to figure out her last days." I offered a sympathetic smile.

"I was filing some stuff for them because they pay me under the table and I'm saving..." she stopped in mid-sentence, "I didn't mean to say pay me under the table."

"Honey, Kenni isn't the IRS." Angela laughed. "We told her not to tell anyone we were paying her cash to work here without filling out a W-2 form. She's saving to join a sorority because we heard they can be very expensive."

"Good for you. I'm glad you're getting paid under the table. I had a job like that when I was your age. If you can believe it, it was to help my Poppa who was sheriff at the time." I was trying hard to help her feel less scared because I could see her hands trembling.

"Go on, Beka," Angela encouraged her.

"Anyways, I guess that Sean was mad about her and Manuel going over the data on their personal time. He'd turned off their data and when Leighann had stayed at home, she couldn't text Manuel in the night. Since his mama's been sick, Manuel didn't want to talk to wake her." Beka cleared her throat. "The next day after school, she told me about it and that her dad told her that day that if she wanted full data then she needed to move out or pay them rent."

"What day was this?" I asked.

"It was the last day of school before Christmas break last week." As she talked, I made notes in my notebook. I was going to tape her but I figured she'd really freak at that. "I told my mom that we couldn't let Leighann live in her car."

"What made you think she was going to live in her car?" I questioned.

"Because she said that Juanita had told Manuel she couldn't live there." Beka looked down at her fingers. She picked at her hangnails. "Leighann said that she and Manuel didn't have a lot of money. She didn't say why, but Jonathon told me that every cent Manuel made went to the family."

"All of this is just awful." Angela's voice cracked. "I didn't want to overstep my bounds, but I went to Jilly. That's when she told me Sean had been abusive and that she'd talked to a lawyer."

"What did she want with a lawyer?" The obvious was divorce, but what about the business?

"She didn't say divorce, but she did say that she wanted to know the particulars of business and what her role would be if they did get a divorce." Her eyes dipped with sadness.

Heaviness settled in my chest. The temperature in the room seemed to have dropped ten degrees with the goosebumps that collected on my arms.

"How did you know Jilly went to see a lawyer?" I asked.

"You don't work with men that drive tow trucks as one of only two women without the two of you becoming friends. It's been a hard road on Jilly. She came to my house and noticed Leighann's car there. I had to tell her that Leighann had been staying the night with me because I loved Leighann too and I couldn't imagine putting Beka out." Angela sucked in a deep breath.

"Do you think that Sean found out about Jilly talking to a lawyer?" I asked. "It wasn't like she didn't cover up meeting with Wally Lamb at Ben's Diner."

"She didn't seem to think Sean knew because Sean never goes into town unless he's got a tow job." She shook her head.

"Is that all?" Beka asked. "I'd like to finish so I can get to the tree lot."

"Yeah, I hear Coach gives you gift certificates." I wanted to break the tension Beka was probably feeling from being asked questions by the sheriff. It could be a little intimidating.

"Aren't you forgetting to tell Sheriff Lowry something?" Angela didn't let her off that easy. "This is very important, Beka. It's okay."

"I'd overheard Leighann screaming at Sean saying that she

was going to find her real father. Then he told her that she was trash just like her real dad and she was ungrateful. They got into a big fight, that's when I snuck away so they wouldn't see me," her voice trailed off.

"Thank you, Beka. I know this was very hard, but you are doing a good thing for Leighann. You were a good friend to her." My greatest fear about Sean was starting to come to light and it appeared he was more of a suspect than he was this morning.

"Is that all?" Angela asked.

"What about those files? Do you keep a log when all the trucks go out, even at night?" I asked.

"I sure do. If there's a service call say in the middle of the night, there is a log in the trucks and the drivers will bring that in to me to log. It's all for tax purposes and liability. Every tow has to be accountable," she said.

"Can you tell me if there was a tow on the night of Leighann's murder?" I asked.

"Sure, but I don't think there was." She walked over to her desk and flipped through the binder. "I just logged in yesterday's." She dragged her finger down one of the pages and shook her head. "Mmm...nope." Her lips pinched, she looked up at me.

"Do you have a running total on a spreadsheet for all the trucks in use?" I asked.

"Of course," she confirmed and pulled another paper off her desk. "Here are the trucks we've been using this month. We rotate trucks since we have to keep them serviced. These five are the ones we are using now. Especially since the blizzard is coming and they've got the winterized package on them."

I didn't know or care to know what the winterized package was, because I refused to believe there was going to be a winter blizzard.

"Can I go take a look at the trucks and compare the mileage to make sure they match?" I asked.

If my theory about someone, whether it was Sean Graves or not, drugged Leighann and after she'd crashed, they'd towed her car to the boat dock, and it went right along with what Stinnett had seen, then one of these trucks had to have been used.

"No problem." She walked over to what I thought was an electrical box and opened it. "I've got to grab the keys. We don't have any on tow right now, so we are good."

She plucked five sets of keys from the box and brought them over to me with the piece of paper.

"The vin number for the trucks are right here on the spread sheet. It coordinates with the number here on the key chain. You'll find the match on the outside right bumper of the truck." She handed them to me.

"Thanks. I really appreciate this." I was so glad she didn't pull that warrant crap on me. "I'll be back shortly."

The trucks were lined up facing the drive, ready to go at the call. I looked at the bumper first and then got the keys. The first three matched the mileage and I was getting a little bit discouraged until I got into the fourth tow truck and the mileage didn't match. My hands shook and my throat dried.

"Back here, Kenni-Bug." I heard Poppa call to me from outside the truck.

I got out of the tow truck and saw Poppa pointing to the back where the chains would've wrapped around the car it was towing. There was red chipped paint on them.

"That's those strange marks." Poppa nodded.

I walked over to my Jeep and grabbed my camera out of my bag. After I turned it on, I flipped through to the photos I'd taken at S&S Auto. Frank had pointed out to me the chipped off paint before I could even investigate it since he had to fill out the information on the cars they tow so there's no damage made by them.

"Just what I thought." Poppa stood over my shoulder and looked at the camera as I compared the marks side-by-side.

"I just can't believe it." I dragged my phone out of my pocket and dialed Finn.

"Any news?" Finn asked.

"Yeah. I'm going to bring in Sean Graves after he gets back from the memorial, but I'm going to go ahead and tape off the house and business." I swallowed, hard. "I think we have crime scene one."

"We sure do." Poppa ghosted into the house and would get started on looking around.

"Do you want some help?" Finn asked.

"If you don't mind sending Scott out to Chimney Rock and log the miles from there to Graves Towing, that'd be great." I gave Finn a quick explanation. "I'll also let him take over and I'll finish up talking to Dr. Shively before I bring him in. I'm going to send Angela Durst and her daughter on home." There was a sick feeling in my stomach.

"My news isn't any better." There was little hope in Finn's voice. "Leighann's phone records came back and there wasn't anything out of the ordinary."

"Nothing seems to surprise me anymore." My head started to hurt thinking about what was going to happen in Cottonwood once everyone heard that Sean Graves was our number one suspect.

It was also so easy nowadays to try and convict someone before they were really in front of a jury, but the evidence was so strong against Sean Graves that I too had even had him locked up in a state penitentiary for murder.

"If we can get this behind us, we can take the next week off for some much-needed time." Finn's words comforted me before we said our goodbyes, it was the grey clouds that appeared to be moving in that worried me.

Chapter Fifteen

Angela Durst had already left before Scott had gotten there. I'd kept my mouth shut so she wouldn't go and squeal to anyone at the memorial since she and Beka were headed there after work. Scott recorded the exact mileage the tow truck was over and not been reported.

"If Sean Graves didn't drive this truck out to the river, I don't know who did." There was a grave look on Scott's face.

"It makes me sick." I shook my head and grabbed the big round keychain out of my bag.

Scott and I had used the bump key to jimmy the lock to the house and the shop since they were combined.

Scott had taped off the property while I headed in to see what Poppa had found.

"Those are Leighann's journals. They date back years and years of abuse from Sean." Poppa had discovered multiple notebooks in Leighann's childhood home. "She knew from a long time ago that she was adopted."

"This was a shocker to me. It had to be the best kept secret in Cottonwood," I said of the unusual nature of it.

"Secrets always make their way out of the woodwork." Poppa had told me that several times but this time he was spot on. "Leighann and Sean were on thin ice."

"The night of the Christmas Cantata, he was aggravated with her because she was there with Manuel having a good time. She didn't even let it bother her that she was having these issues." I started to play the back and forth game we loved to play.

"When she got home, they ended up having another fight and she brought up the fact he wasn't her father." Poppa paced back and forth as the scene unfolded before us.

"She continued to threaten him about how he wasn't her father and he felt she was ungrateful, using his medication to poison her." I wasn't really sure how that fit in, but I threw it in there.

"How did he get her to drive to Chimney Rock?" Poppa asked a question I'd yet to even mull over since I'd seen the whole mileage thing.

"He told her that Manuel had called," I said not so convinced that's how it happened. "He knew she'd jump in her car to go after Manuel and just to be sure he followed her."

"There's only one way to find out." Poppa was right. "Bring him in."

"Not without crossing all my I's and T's just yet. I've got some time to get over to Dr. Shively's to talk to her before they get back from the funeral home." I pulled my phone out of my pocket. "Just for good measure, I'll call Max Bogus to give me a heads up when it's over and they're leaving. I'll come back here to get him."

"You leaving the new kid here?" Poppa asked.

"I sure am." I headed on back out of the house and gave Scott some specific instructions on what I wanted bagged up. The journals and the pills for sure.

I gripped the Wagoneer's steering wheel when I pushed the pedal all the way to the floor. Rarely did I ever go over the speed limit and when I did, it was with my siren on. I had some ground to cover before Leighann's memorial was over. Max told me that the memorial was going well and he'd call me when Sean and Jilly were about to leave. There were some kids Leighann had gone to high school with and the line was longer than they'd anticipated even though there was no body to see.

Since it was already in the middle of the day, I'd hoped people might've cancelled any appointments they'd had with Camille Shively and she'd have an open window to discuss Sean Graves and the prescription. In light of the current evidence against Sean, I still wanted to talk to her about Juanita Liberty's Crohn's condition.

The waiting room was empty like I'd hoped. I walked up to the receptionist window.

"Sheriff." Her eyes drew down my nose. "I'm assuming you're here on official business."

"That's right. Camille is expecting me." I stood there gripping my bag and watched her rush off.

I turned around and faced the small brown leather loveseats and perfectly matched end tables. Framed photos of Camille in her graduation cap and gown decorated with all sorts of colored cords hung on the walls. They represented just how smart she was in her class. The all-important piece of paper that told us she that she was in fact a doctor was proudly displayed.

The doctor's office was already an unnerving place to be when you had an appointment and I could tell that Camille had taken great lengths to make the office homier to help get rid of the white coat syndrome.

The water feature in the corner tickled a soothing sound. I

couldn't help but wonder if Camille had strategically placed it there since it was the latest rage in battling anxiety. I could tell her that it wasn't working for me. The more I thought about Sean Graves and what I was about to arrest him for was stress beyond the normal. Stress came with the job, but when a father figure was accused of such a horrific crime, the level of anxiety was almost unbearable.

Before I could even sit down, Camille was at the door in her doctor's whites, looking very much like the girl next door that made her clients feel comfortable with her. Her long black hair was pulled into a low ponytail at the nape of her neck. Her pale face softened as she smiled.

"Kenni." She held the waiting room door for me. "Let's go back to my office."

"Thanks for seeing me." I unzipped my bag and had the papers that she'd requested all ready for her. "Here's the request for subpoena."

"I can tell you that Sean Graves isn't a man that appears to be anxious or even unstable. He's got some anger issues that we are working through, but if you think he killed his daughter, I'm going to strongly tell you that in my professional opinion, he did not." Camille didn't even give me a chance to ask her any questions before she started right on in as though she'd already rehearsed it.

"Professional opinion? *Pweft.*" Poppa appeared next to Camille, blowing her off. "She needs to stick to doctoring and not policing."

"He'd been having some trouble sleeping the past couple of weeks because he and Jilly are having some issues coming to agreement with how to handle Leighann's decisions as an adult, but now they have a whole set of different issues they are going to have to face," she said.

"He's got a lot of issues, lady." Poppa rocked back on his heels. "You need to give her something to chew on."

"I appreciate your professional opinion, but the evidence speaks for itself and right now it's screaming that Sean Graves murdered his stepdaughter." My words caught me off-guard. I'd never called Leighann his step-daughter and it did make the awful crime more realistic and believable rather than calling her his daughter. "Her car was towed into the river. She was floating in the back and the keys were in her pocket. The mileage log on his tow truck just so happens to be the exact mileage from his shop to the river."

"Weee-dogggy." Poppa smacked his knee in delight. "Look at that shocked look on her face."

I literally had to suck in a deep breath to keep from saying too much. So I went in for the kill.

"I'm going to need copies of all of your records on Sean Grave as well as the prescriptions because Leighann was given Ambien before she was murdered," my words were met with the good doctor's jaw dropping.

"I'm..." she stammered, "I...um..." She looked away and cleared her throat. "I had no idea. He seemed genuinely concerned about Leighann's future."

"It appears that Juanita Liberty was the same way. And I'd like to know about her Crohn's disease." I watched Camille write on a piece of paper. "I know that I have to have all my I's and T's crossed with solid evidence that Sean Graves had anything to do with Leighann's murder. From what I've heard, Juanita is battling Crohn's disease. She felt the same way about Leighann as Sean did Manuel. She too had motive to kill Leighann, but she was at home ill the night of Leighann's murder, so technically she's not a suspect. But I'd like to know if she's as bad off as they say."

"I'm assuming you'd get a warrant for that too." Camille pushed a button on her phone and called for the secretary. "She does have Crohn's. We are working with a specialist on various treatments but until it's under control with all the new meds, then I'd say she's a little touch and go. We've been treating it for years, but now we are having to use some experimental things."

The secretary walked over to Camille and took the sticky note she'd written on.

"I need all the files copied," she looked up at the secretary under raised brows. The secretary hurried out.

"I'm sorry to hear that. She's got a few young children." My heart ached for Manuel.

I couldn't imagine what was going through his young mind and sympathized with how he was going to have to take care of his mother once her disease progressed.

My phone chirped a text. I dragged it out of my pocket and read it from Max.

"Did Juanita happen to take Ambien?" I asked just to make sure.

"No. She's already tired enough without needing a sleep aid," she confirmed.

"I've got to go." I stood up. "Do you think she's done with the copies?"

"She should be." Camille stood up too. "I'm sorry about my thoughts about Sean. I guess it goes to prove that you don't know someone by what they tell you."

"He's not tried and convicted yet." I reminded her and left the office, grabbing the files from the secretary on my way out.

"Good boy," I pat Duke on the head when I got back into

the Jeep.

"What are you waiting on?" Poppa tapped the dashboard with his fingers. "Get a move on it. We've got an arrest to make."

I took a couple of deep breaths before I turned the engine over.

"Well? What are you waiting for?" Poppa asked. He hit the dash a little harder this time. "Go!"

"Poppa, weren't you the one who told me that I better make sure because I just can't go off and accuse people of crimes they didn't commit?" I asked.

"Yes, I did, Kenni-Bug." His chin lifted up and then down in a definitive yes. "What more evidence do you need? He has a prescription of Ambien. He has a history of abusing the poor girl. His tow truck matches up to what happened to the SUV in the river. He flew off the handle when she told him she was going to find her real father. He also had to've found out that Jilly was going to leave him. That does a lot to a man."

"You're right. We can't make the evidence up. These are all facts and it all points to Leighann's death." A lump so dry formed in my throat and I could barely swallow to make it wet.

Instead of fighting the fear inside, I simply put the Jeep in drive and headed right on back to Graves Towing to do one of the hardest arrests I've ever had to do.

Chapter Sixteen

"Kenni, won't you come in?" Jilly held the door open for me to enter.

"I appreciate that, but I'm here to see Sean." My face set stern, my eyes had a softness to them as they looked at the wife and mother who was about to lose everything. My heart ached for her, but I had a job to do and bringing Leighann's killer to justice was my only concern.

"Kenni. Honey." Sean walked up and stood over her shoulder. "Is everything okay?"

"Can I see you outside?" I questioned.

"It's awful cold and we really just want to get some rest. If you've got some information, come on in and we can talk over coffee." Jilly still continued to try to get me inside. "The Sweet Adelines left so much coffee cake and we've got to eat it."

"I think she wants to talk to me." Sean moved past Jilly and stepped outside. It was easy enough for me to size him up when my head came up to his chin.

"Yep. About the same distance from the pedals in Leighann's car to the seat." Poppa had noticed what I'd noticed. "Oh, Kenni-Bug." The tone in his voice didn't make me feel any better. "You've got your work cut out for you."

"You got the killer, didn't you?" Sean looked down at me.

"Yes," I choked out and then cleared my throat. "Sean Graves," My chin lifted into the air, my voice loud and clear, I said, "You are under arrest for the murder of Leighann Graves."

"What?" He drew back. I stood firm. "You've lost your mind!" His boisterous voice blew past me and it was so powerful, it almost knocked me over.

"Anything you say can and will be used against you." I reached around my utility belt and unclipped my cuffs.

"I'm not going," he protested and chuckled. "You're crazy."

"Sean? Kenni?" Jilly stood at the door. The cup of coffee she had in her hands shattered on the front porch when she dropped it. "No, Sean, no," she pleaded and shook her head. The tears began to flood down her face. "Not my baby. You killed my baby?"

"No." He pointed to Jilly and then pointed to me. "You are wrong. Very wrong."

"I'm taking you down to the department." I reached for his wrist. "If I'm wrong, we can sort it out down there."

"We are going to sort this out," he demanded. "Jilly, woman, get yourself together. You hear me?" He hollered.

"You've man-handled her long enough." I clipped the cuffs on him a little tighter than I'd normally done. "I can't wait to see you behind bars."

"Kenni, stay calm. Just do your job." Poppa ghosted past me towards the Jeep. "Get him in the Wagoneer and let's do the job."

"Jilly, call Wally Lamb!" He had one good scream before I shoved him in the back seat of the Wagoneer.

I'd like to say there was complete silence or even some sort of sadness on the way back into town, but he was just piss and vinegar the entire way.

"You think you're going to get re-elected, you're crazy. I don't care who I have to throw money towards to beat you right out of office, but I'll donate today." He spewed hate words the whole way there. "Too bad you're not like Elmer."

"Sean, I'm telling you to stop talking," I warned him.

"Are you going to take my right to talk away too?" He asked sarcastically.

I gripped the wheel so hard that by the time I'd parked the Jeep in the alley behind the department, my fingers were numb and tingling.

"Finn," I called after I'd beeped in my walkie-talkie. "Can you come get Sean out of my Jeep?"

He didn't even answer back. He bolted out the door. When I got out, our eyes met. There was an unspoken word between us. He knew he had to give me a few minutes to collect myself and I knew it too.

"Betty, I'm going to go to the bathroom and get a coffee. Please make Sean comfortable." I didn't look at her. I unzipped my coat and hung it up on the coat tree.

"Wally Lamb is on his way," Betty warned as I pushed through the door between the department and Cowboy's Catfish. "And your mama dropped off a casserole for you to take to Manuel Liberty. She said something about how he's grieving too."

The bathroom light flickered above my head as I stood at the sink, grasping the edges. My stomach hurt, and I felt like I was going to be sick. I just couldn't believe that Sean Graves had been given the precious gift of having a wonderful daughter and took her life.

"Over what?" I looked hard into my own eyes in the mirror.

"What did you kill her over?" I asked myself like I was going to ask him.

Only the hint of tears burned the top of my nose. I knew I had get a grip before I could go in there and interrogate him when Wally Lamb got there.

I turned on the cold-water knob and let it run for a few minutes to get good and cold. I bent my head overtop the sink and used my hands to splash water on my face.

"Ding, ding," Poppa pretend to ring the bell. He pinched a faint smile. "These are the tough times," he reminded me. "You've got to remember all the good. All the donations you do during the year. All the volunteer hours. The citizens who drop by and bring you pies just to thank you. The sticker badges you put in the smallest hands of Cottonwood that look up to you and when they grow up they want to be sheriff. Those are the events you have to remember to get you through the bad times like this one."

"Sean Graves?" I still questioned with disbelief. "It's so unthinkable. All the times I went to bat for him and all the times we used his towing company." I shook my head and used my sleeve to wipe off any left-over water.

"You and I both know that people lose their minds and do things that are out of their character, but now that the spotlight has been bright on Sean Graves, I think you know deep down that he didn't lose his mind." Poppa jabbed his finger towards my heart. "He's been down-right ornery for a while, only behind closed doors."

I wiped my face one more time and shook my head.

"You're right." I sucked in a deep breath. "I really wish you were here."

"I am here. Right here next to you," he assured me.

"Will you make sure I ask the appropriate questions?" I knew when I proceeded with Wally Lamb there as I questioned Sean, Wally would try and turn every question into a debate.

"I'll be right there." He nodded.

There was a sense of light that passed between us that gave me a confidence that I'd dug down deep to get. I was ready to bring Leighann's killer to justice.

Chapter Seventeen

"Sheriff Lowry, I think you've gone on an all-out hunting spree since you're trying to bolt out of town with your boyfriend." Wally Lamb slid his shifty eyes toward Deputy Finn Vincent. "You haven't even taken the time to properly investigate this case in the last what," he see-sawed his hand, "forty-eight hours, seventy-two hours?"

He drew back, duck-billed his lips and gave me a geesh look.

"Am I right or am I right?" He asked and sauntered over to the cell. "I'm going to have to ask you to let my client go. Now, open the cell."

"Listen here," Finn took a step forward.

"I've got it." I shot Finn a look. "I'm just waiting for Mr. Lamb to finish before I tell him how this is going to go."

"Is that right?" Wally Lamb asked and folded his arms across his chest over his fancy suit.

"That's right. I've arrested your client and if you'd like to stay for some questioning, you may do so per the law." I grabbed a tape recorder out of my desk drawer. "This is my domain. I was elected by our peers and citizens to do a job. I'm going to do that job whether you, Mr. Lamb, like it or not."

"Fine. Proceed," he said with a smirk. "Don't worry," he assured Sean.

"If I was alive, I'd show that boy how to treat a woman and use good manners." Poppa huffed and puffed.

"Scott, can you pull the desk closer to Mr. Graves?" I didn't want it all to be so formal, but Wally left me with no choice. Finn helped him with the desk and finished up by putting the chairs next to the cell.

"Please state your full name," I told Sean after I'd pushed record.

"Sean Howard Graves," he said loud and clear.

"I think we can lose the formalities," I paused to receive an agreement from him. "Can you tell me how it came to be that you adopted Leighann?"

"About eighteen years ago, Jilly had come to town looking for a job. She had an infant daughter. My daddy had an opening in the office and he gave her a job. Over the course of a few years, I'd grown fond of her and Leighann. She'd bring her to the office and my family tended to the baby like she was our own." He took a gulp. "I fell in love with them. When I asked her to marry me, I swear it was the happiest day of my mom's life. She and my dad were so happy."

"I wish I could say that he's putting on an act, but I clearly remember how much they loved her and Leighann. They were happy." Poppa had softened on me.

"Yep, sounds like a killer to me." Wally threw his hands up in the air.

I shot him a look. He turned away from me.

"How long have you been taking Ambien?" I asked.

"Recently after Leighann and I had gotten into a fight and she said she was going to move out, I couldn't sleep because I wasn't sure where she was, and I knew I had to let her fly in order to let her survive." He looked down at his hands as he clasped them together. "I knew where she was the whole time. I would follow her around in my car so I knew she was okay. I even knew that Angela Durst had taken her in. I was waiting her out."

"What about the night of the dance? I saw the look on your face when you saw her and Manuel cozied up next to the punch bowl. You didn't look happy." This was the beginning of the end from what I could tell.

"Leighann had come over to the table upset because Rachel had made fun of her for staying in Cottonwood. I was mad because this was the exact reason I wanted her to go to college and get an education. People made fun of me all my life for taking over my parents' tow company. Even though they need me, they still turn their noses down. I couldn't imagine a world where Leighann would live and her peers treat her badly," his voice trailed off.

"That does make sense," Poppa said and made me wonder whose side he was on. What happened to him telling me that he'd have my back when I was in the bathroom?

"When Leighann got home, you and she had a fight. She said she was going to find out who her real dad was and you got mad, slipped her one or two of your sleeping pills before you let her get into her car and drive off." My voice escalated before I went in for the kill, "When you realized she didn't die in the crash, you drove your tow truck, put her car in the river after you'd unbuckled her and put her keys in her pocket."

"Are you crazy?" He jumped up and squeezed his face in between the bars.

"Sheriff, you have a very active imagination." Wally clapped his hands. "I'm gonna have to give you an award for a big imagination."

"How do you explain the fact that her car seat was pushed back to the exact height you'd be sitting down or the exact distance you've got between the pedals on your personal tow truck to the seat? It's the exact same measurements." I opened the folder and took out the photos and the measurements from both. "And how do you explain this?"

"What is that?" Wally picked up the photo I'd taken from the mileage log and the photo of the odometer from his tow truck.

"Mr. Graves's tow truck that he uses wasn't logged properly. The missing miles is the exact mileage it takes from his shop to Chimney Rock and back." I smacked my hand on the desk.

"Wally? Aren't you going to stop her?" Sean protested, shaking the bars.

"Sean Graves, you got mad at Leighann for wanting to search for her father. You got mad at Jilly for filing for divorce and you were seeking revenge. Jilly even said you two'd not been sleeping in the same bed. You killed Leighann Graves and you just need to save the poor citizens our tax dollars and just admit it." I didn't let up.

"Bravo!" Wally Lamb clapped and laughed. "Like I said, you have a very active imagination. Now, if you don't mind. I think Betty said we've got a bond hearing."

Betty sat bug-eyed and speechless at her desk with her mouth dropped wide open. Slowly she nodded. Her mouth closed, opened, closed and popped open again.

"That's it?" Sean looked between me and Wally Lamb. "You're not going to say anything?"

"I've got plenty to say. Before the judge." Wally tipped his head. "See you in a couple of hours."

There was complete silence until Wally Lamb walked out of the door.

"That's it?" Sean shoved off the bars. "What kind of coo-coo lawyer is he?"

"He's right." I walked back over to the cell. "The judge will give you a bond and Wally will bond you out. Then he'll start to put together a case for you."

Not that I wanted to let Sean know anything, but he did still have rights.

"Kenni, do you honestly think I killed Leighann?" He eased down on the cot. "The night she went missing, I told you that I went to Chimney Rock to look for her. I didn't go that night. I jumped into my tow that morning after Manuel came by saying she wasn't with him. I'd completely forgotten to put the mileage in the log." He bent over and rested his forearms on his thighs. "Jilly and I had been going to marriage counseling. She met with Wally Lamb at Ben's Diner to tell him that we were staying together and not going through the divorce."

"That's good to hear." Poppa was a sucker. He ghosted himself next to Sean on the cot. "Poor Jilly has been through enough."

It took everything in my person not to just fly off the handle at Poppa, but I couldn't risk everyone seeing me and thinking I was the unhinged person in the room.

"We left the dance and that night I slept in our marital bed. You can ask Jilly. I didn't move until Manuel knocked on the door. I didn't kill Leighann. I loved her. I raised her. And I'm not proud of the wrongful things I've done to my wife and daughter, but I am seeking help for that." He wiped his hand across his face and dropped his chin to his chest. "I love my girls."

"He didn't do it." Poppa hopped up. "Go back and talk to the Liberty boy." Poppa tapped his temple. "Something ain't right. Something's off."

Chapter Eighteen

"Sheriff, what are you doing here?"

I was surprised to see Beka Durst answer the Liberty's front door. By the look on her face, she was as surprised as me.

"What are you doing here?" I asked her back.

"I'm waiting on the Libertys to get back from the memorial. I told them I'd hang out here." She shrugged.

"I'm shocked you're not at the memorial," I said and wondered why the Libertys were still at the memorial when Sean and Jilly had gone home and I'd arrested him.

"I'm not really good with all that dead stuff. I mean, I loved Leighann and all, but it wasn't like we were great friends." Her eyes slid down to the casserole carrier.

"I'm dropping off one of Mama's chicken pot pies." I held the handles of Mama's casserole carrier that she made during a craft night at Lulu's boutique. "Do you mind if I put it in the kitchen?" I asked because if I didn't take it out of the carrier and bring it back to Mama, she'd freak out.

"Not at all. They've been getting a bunch of food." She walked away from the door and I walked in. "Everyone feels bad for Manuel. It wasn't like they were married or anything."

"Are you friends with Jonathan?" I asked, knowing that she

was a senior and so was Jonathan, figuring they were in class together. Plus, I'd seen them at the tree farm.

"Ummm." She shrugged again on the way to the kitchen. "Not really. I was more friends with Manuel than Jonathan. That is, before he started dating Leighann."

Okay, I wondered to myself, did she have a thing for Manuel? I let the thoughts swirl around in my head like they were marinating while I sat the casserole carrier on the kitchen table and took out the foil pan with Mama's chicken pot pie in it. There was book bag next to a monogrammed purse with Beka's initials on it. Upon deeper inspection, something else in her bag caught my eye.

"It's great that you're here for Manuel," I said, stopping Beka in her tracks. "Is that your purse?"

"Mmmhmmmm," she hummed. "Juanita got it for me from Lulu's Boutique. I mean, Mrs. Liberty."

"I really like it." I picked it up to disguise that I wanted to knock over the bag and see if I saw what I thought I saw. "I'm so sorry," I gasped for effect when the bag went tumbling to the ground when I picked up the purse. All the contents fell out, even the emergency kit with Leighann's initials on it.

She scurried over and tried to grab all the contents and throw it back in the bag. I snatched the first aid kit from her.

"Who knows, maybe the two of you can date now that Leighann is out of the way." I held up the kit in front of her face.

My body language reading skills kicked in, but so did Poppa's commentary.

"Did you see that?" Poppa appeared next to Beka. "Her jaw. It tensed. And... "he pointed at her. "Her chest is rising."

"His mother would like that," she said in a low voice as she stood up. "Juanita didn't like Leighann. Neither did Manuel's brothers. She really didn't deserve him."

"That's why you killed her, so you could date him." The pieces were falling into place, though when I sized her up, she wasn't as tall as my calculation from where the seat in Leighann's SUV had been moved. "You had access to Graves Towing and the Ambien prescribed to Leighann's dad."

"I don't mean no disrespect." Beka opened a counter drawer and shuffled through it like she was looking for something. "I don't think you understand the connection me and Manuel had before Leighann came along."

"Why don't we head on down to the station and sort this out?" Now I wished I'd had on my uniform or at least my gun strapped on my utility belt instead of in my bag, which did me no good since I left it in the Wagoneer.

"No, I can't do that." Her eyes darted around the room. "I mean," her head twitched, "you obviously know."

"What do I know?" I questioned so she'd calm down. She looked like a cat in a roomful of rocking chairs.

"You know I killed her." Her shaky hand outstretched in front of her as she pointed at me.

"I'm not sure of it. And if you did, I'm sure we can work this out." I took a step towards her. "I get it. You were, are, in love with Manuel. Trust me." I put my hand in the air when I noticed she shuffled to the opposite side of me. I wanted to gain her trust. "If someone tried to take Finn away from me." I shook my head. "I don't know what I'd do."

"She wasn't taking him from me. I was taking back what's mine. What we used to have before she flaunted herself at him at the towing company after he'd found out his mama was sick." She started to cry. "Juanita had told me that she wished he'd dated me. All those times Sean kept Leighann away from

Manuel, Manuel came to me." Beka's nose flared as the words came out of her gritted teeth. "He told me that we could go off to college and forget this town. I had it all planned out."

"Did the two of you date?" I asked, trying to bide the time for her to get comfortable with me.

"No, but we would've if it weren't for her. I'd given her a few months to show her nasty side to him. When she decided not to go to college, I knew that I had to get a plan to set him free. If she wasn't around, we could get out of Cottonwood and begin our lives."

She walked over to the window to look out.

It was a perfect opportunity to slip my phone out of my pocket and quickly hit Finn's phone number. "Manuel and his family will be back soon. I need to be sure I'm here for him and continue my plan."

"He's going to need you." I'd slipped the phone with the speaker side up in my front pocket. "The Sweet Adelines will probably be stopping by soon."

"Those nosy old coots." Beka rolled her eyes.

"They are, but they have a good heart, just like you." I tried to soften my facial features, so she'd start to trust me, but the fact I was the law wasn't helping none. "I just don't understand how you did it."

"Leighann was upset and I texted her to meet me at her house. I'd gotten my mom's keys to the towing company and knew if I could get in there, I'd be able to get Sean's sleeping pills." She smiled, her eyes narrowed, and it made me sick to my stomach. "Kids nowadays are soft. You know? They like to take the easy way out. I knew if it came out that Sean was abusive, and she and Manuel were having problems, then it was a no brainer to look like she'd hurt herself."

"So, she slipped her a mickey, huh." Poppa swept up next to her and got real close. "How did she get the car in the lake?" Poppa asked.

"Exactly how did the SUV get into the water?" I asked.

"I'd seen her throw her phone at Manuel when she got mad and left the Moose. I knew she didn't have it on her. I asked Manuel to get her a fountain Cherry Coke from Ben's since it was her favorite and when she came to his house, she'd be all goo-goo eyed. Little did they know that I'd been to Ben's earlier with my mom and gotten a Cherry Coke fountain drink with no ice to-go. Cherry Coke was Leighann's favorite. When she showed up to meet me at her house, I'd already slipped a couple of the sleeping pills in her drink." There was a certain look of pride on her face as if she'd completely gotten away with it.

"After we talked, I pretended to get a text on my cell and told her it was Manuel. He said that if I'd seen her to tell her to go to Chimney Rock like they used to when they were younger. It was their secret rendezvous place." She crossed her hands to her heart. "It was a perfect place for her to die and now we can have our own rendezvous spot."

"She drove there?" I still hadn't connected how the back-side panel had been found so far down the road.

"I didn't realize how fast the sleeping pill was going to work. My plan changed after I followed behind her to Chimney Rock. She fell asleep at the wheel and when the car went around one of the curves, it went off the road and bumped a tree just enough for the panel to fall off." She rolled her eyes. "Her stupid car was stuck."

"Did that kill her?" I asked.

"No," she said abruptly. "If it had, I'd've left her there. But I had to make sure she was good and dead. That's when I decided that I was going to have to put her in the river. I drove back to her house and used my mom's keys to get into the tow company where I got keys to one of the tow trucks. It actually turned out better than my original plan because I loaded her car up on the tow and then just backed up on the boat ramp and dumped the entire car in the river."

"That's why the car seat was moved so far back because this here nut job is taller than Leighann." Poppa was standing next to her sizing her up. "You can take her. She's a pipsqueak."

"You moved her out of the driver's seat?" I asked, hoping all the details were going on the recorder of the phone.

"I shoved her after I got the car towed to the boat dock." Beka tsked.

"What is it with these young kids today? Just want what they want and take it," Poppa said with a disgusted tone.

"How did the keys get in her pocket?" I asked.

"That was a bit of a rookie move on my end," she said nonchalantly like we were just two buddies having an afternoon sweet tea. "Before I went to get the tow truck, I turned off the car so no one would see the exhaust because it's so cold with that storm coming."

"There's not going to be a storm!" My voice escalated. I was sick and tired of hearing this junk about the storm. Apparently, my voice scared her and she ran past me, shoving me to the side.

"Don't make me do this!" I yelled, running after her.

It was the worst thing in the world to get into a pursuit and with a kid.

Before she'd made it to the front door, I leapt into the air and tackled her to the ground.

She was sobbing, but I had to hold her like a tied hog or she'd run again. I flipped her over to her front and with my knee jammed deep in her back, I realized I didn't have my cuffs. Quickly I looked around and saw the coat tree. I jerked a belt from one of the coats and used it to wrap around her tiny wrists.

She was just a kid. Too bad, she had her whole life in front of her until this crime of passion over took her sense of emotions.

"Beka Durst, I'm arresting you for the murder of Leighann Graves. Do you understand me?" I asked her. There was nothing but sobs escaping her limp body. "You have the right to remain silent, though I've got it all on my phone. Anything you say can and will certainly be used against you in the court of law." I jerked her up to stand and continued reading her the Miranda rights. I grabbed my phone off the floor on our way out.

With one hand, I gripped her arm and the other had my phone.

"Did you get all that?" I asked Finn.

"I'm on my way to the Libertys' right now." He clicked off and I slipped the phone back in my pocket.

We headed out of the Libertys' front door just as Manuel and his family were piling out of the family van.

"Now, I've got to get you down to the station." I opened the back door of the Wagoneer and helped her inside.

"It's only because I love you Manuel Liberty!" She screamed before I slammed the door, not caring a bit if the glass window smacked her in the nose. "I'd do anything for you!"

"What's going on here?" Juanita Liberty strutted up to the Jeep with all her sons in tow.

"We have a confession. Leighann Graves was murdered by Beka Durst because she was jealous of their relationship and is in love with your son." My eyes slid past her shoulder and caught Manuel's face. "I'm sorry, you'll have to wait outside until Deputy Vincent comes to clear the scene."

Manuel's eyes slowly closed shut as his chin fell to his chest.

"Good work, Sheriff," was all that Juanita Liberty could muster up before she gestured for her boys to wait by the car.

"Manuel! Manuel!" Beka's voice was distorted by the glass between her and the world as she desperately tried to get Manuel to look at her when he walked by. "Tell him how much I love him, Juanita!"

I looked around for Poppa as I walked in front of the Jeep to get inside and haul her down to the one department cell, but he wasn't around.

"Silent night, holy night," the radio played when I started up the Jeep.

"Turn this crap off," Beka said snidely.

I turned it up and smiled.

"This is for you, Poppa." I sucked in a deep breath and put the gear shift in drive.

Chapter Nineteen

"You let my baby go, Kenni Lowry!" Angela Durst had run into the sheriff's department with Wally Lamb on her heels.

"Let me take care of this because it seems that our good sheriff here is going to arrest everyone in Cottonwood for Leighann's death." Wally stuck his arm out, stopping Angela from going after me. Or it appeared she was gunning for me. "Kenni, um, Sheriff, on what grounds do you believe you can arrest my client?"

"On the grounds that she is in love with Manuel Liberty and out of a crime of passion she killed Leighann Graves to get her out of the way so she, herself, could live happily ever after with Manuel." I stated the obvious.

"Not to mention that she confessed and happened to have the missing contents from Leighann's car in her possession," Scott finished up.

"She's a minor and I want her out of that jail cell right now," Wally Lamb said with a stern voice. "And Sean too."

"I have no clue what's going on." Sean sat stunned on the edge of the cot.

"Beka confessed to killing Leighann. She's got all the details." I grabbed the cell keys out of my drawer and went over to unlock it. Scott stepped in and took Sean by the arm. "Sean, you can come out."

"Thank God." He stood up and turned to face Beka. "After everything I did for you and your mother, you killed my daughter?"

"Beka, you tell her right now the truth." Angela rushed over to the cell and gripped the bars, staring at the young girl who had replaced Sean on the cot. "Beka, I know you didn't do this. You were home." Angela's jaw dropped, and she swiveled around on the balls of her feet. "She was at home watching a movie with me. She went to the dance but had to be home by curfew."

"Mama, hush. I did it. I drugged and killed Leighann." She bolted off the cot and stood ramrod straight with her fists to her side. "I killed her! I killed her!"

"She didn't kill no one." Poppa appeared cross-legged on the cot, nearly making me faint.

Why was Poppa back? What in the world was going on? Had I just hauled in a teenager for a murder she'd not committed? What was I thinking?

"Wait." I stopped them from talking and that included Poppa. I had to have a clear head. "You said that you texted Leighann to meet you at her house." I recalled what she'd said about how she lured Leighann that night. "But Manuel had her phone, so how did she get your text?"

"Shut up! I did it!" She screamed through gritted teeth.

"Give me a minute with her, please." I put my hand out to everyone.

"Is she covering up for something Manuel had done?" Poppa stared at Beka who was suddenly on the floor in fetal position, repeating that she'd killed her over and over.

"Beka." I unlocked the cell and bent down next to her. "This is a very nice jail cell, but if you killed Leighann, I promise that you won't be in a prison anywhere near this nice. Your entire life will be over."

I stroked her hair and tried to comfort her while she sobbed on the floor.

"Love is a very crazy and real thing. Especially at your age. I understand that you are in love with Manuel, but if you are covering up for him for something he's done, that's not love on his part." I continued to talk softly with her and let everyone around me drown out. "You have your entire life ahead of you. Don't you want to join Rachel at State and be in her sorority? Remember all the fun she was telling you about when you two were working the tree lot? If you go to jail, you won't ever go to college. You won't ever have another boyfriend or even get married. Your life will be over. And for what? Manuel will still carry on."

She pushed herself up to sit side-legged on her hip.

"What about a sick person in jail? Will they get medical help then go home?" She questioned with big tears in her eyes.

"Juanita Liberty. Ummm-mmmm," Poppa's lips were pressed together. "She killed that girl. I know it."

"Yes. Like Juanita Liberty?" I asked Beka. "If Juanita killed Leighann, she'd get some medical treatment for her Crohn's and be released." She nodded.

Out of the corner of my eye, I saw Poppa ghost right on up through the ceiling. My heart fell.

"I didn't know she did it until I found Leighann's emergency kit in their house. Juanita walked in and saw me holding it. She's the one who told me how much she loved me and wanted me to be married to Manuel. She said that if it came down to it and I took the fall, I would get off because I'm a minor. No one was going to send a kid to jail. That's what she said." Beka wiped the tears from her eyes. "She said that since she had Crohn's and in the last stages, that she didn't care if she went to jail because she'd die knowing Leighann couldn't hurt her son's future anymore. But if I took the fall..." Her voice trailed off. Angela rushed to the cell bars. Beka looked up at her. "I'm sorry, Mama. I thought I was doing the right thing."

"Beka, honey, she used your lack of knowledge about the disease to get you to take the fall for her dirty work. She's not dying." Her mama tried to tell her daughter how Juanita had manipulated her.

There was some scurrying behind me and I knew it was Scott rushing out the door to bring Juanita Liberty to justice.

"It's going to be okay." I stood up and let Angela come into the cell to console her daughter while I called Finn.

"I'm about all done here," he answered the phone.

"Don't leave. Deputy Lee is on his way over there. Don't say anything until you talk to him when he gets there, but Juanita Liberty is the real killer." My words were met with silence. "Are you there?"

"Yeah. We'll bring her in." He clicked off.

Beka had retracted what she told me and actually had told me the truth, which wasn't far from what she'd confessed. In fact, Juanita had faked sicker than what she was and knew that her son and Leighann had a fight. She also knew that her son would stop at nothing for Leighann and if she ended Leighann's life, she'd be giving Manuel his life back.

"Juanita saw it as a win-win situation. The disease is progressing and she knew that if she was dead and gone, Manuel would marry Leighann and it'd be Leighann that'd move into her house and finish raising Manuel's brothers while Manuel worked. It was a life she didn't want for her boys. In the end, Juanita Liberty couldn't find it within herself to forgive Leighann for helping Manuel make the decision not to go to college, when in fact, it was her sickness that made Manuel's decision easy." I told Mama over supper that night after we'd gotten Juanita placed into custody.

"Juanita had only confessed to Beka after Beka had found Leighann's emergency kit in the Liberty house while visiting. In some sort of sick way, Juanita had told Beka that if need be, Beka should confess to killing Leighann so Juanita could spend what time she had on the earth with her boys. She also gave Beka the permission to live in her house, happily ever after with Manuel," Finn finished up the story while I continued to eat Mama's chicken pot pie that she'd made for me as a special I'm-sorry-for-being-so-crabby-about-Christmas make up.

"Juanita Liberty is really that ill?" Mama asked.

"Yeah, she was hauling them trees like a champion the other day," My dad chimed in between bites.

"Not really. She only told her family that because she needed an excuse to kill Leighann. She had tricked Leighann into talking with her by telling her that Manuel was really upset and she wanted to make amends with her so they could move on." The sadness of it all made a lump in my throat. "Can you imagine the excitement Leighann felt when she thought Manuel's mother had finally come around and their life was going to be happy?"

"Why was Leighann driving?" Mama asked.

"Juanita had originally thought she was just going to shoot Leighann, but when she saw the sleeping pills, she'd made Leighann some water to sip because she was so upset. Then proceeded to tell Leighann that Manuel had made a special night for them down at Chimney Rock boat ramp. Alluding to the fact Manuel had gotten Leighann an engagement ring for Christmas." Finn shrugged. "Leighann jumped in her car and headed that way thinking Manuel was there waiting for her with an engagement ring."

"She followed Leighann to make sure she'd wreck and die, but when Leighann survived the wreck, she remembered seeing the keys to the tow trucks, so Juanita took Leighann's keys back to the tow company, let herself in and took the keys along with Sean's truck so she could easily slip the SUV into the river and bye-bye Leighann." I let out a big long sigh. "Another sick thing she did was take everything out of the Leighann's car because she didn't want anything in there to help Leighann if she woke up."

Everyone looked at me with shocked expressions on their faces.

"Why on earth would Beka try to say that she did it?" Mama asked.

"Beka thought that since she was a minor, that she'd not go to jail if she took the fall and her and Manuel could be happy together."

"I heard her mama is getting her some counseling," Mama chimed in.

"That's good. She needs it." I was happy to hear that.

"That seems like a lot of work to go through because you simply didn't like someone." My dad pushed back from the table.

"You'd be surprised." Finn tweaked a grin. "I've seen so many crimes of passion killings that nothing surprises me now."

"This might surprise you." Dad gave Mama the look. It

wasn't a look that he gave often, but when he did, you knew he meant business.

"What?" My eyes shifted between him and Mama.

"I want to say," *ahem*, Mama cleared her throat. "I'm sorry for the way I've acted over the past few months. It was immature and childish to think my one and only daughter would never leave me on Christmas."

"Vivian," My dad's voice boomed over the table.

"I'm getting there," she told my dad. "Finn, you are a very nice young man. If Kendrick is dating someone and has to visit his family, I couldn't think of a nicer boy we'd like to have her date. With that, I'm asking for your forgiveness."

"Oh, Mama," I gasped and jumped up, running around the family table to give her a hug. "This makes it so much easier on me. Thank you."

"I love you and I want you to go and have a wonderful time." She returned the hug and held it for a long time.

Deep in my soul, I knew everything was going to be okay and the excitement was building up.

"Don't forget to come pick me up," I reminded her that she was going to pick me up in a couple of days to take me to the airport.

Chapter Twenty

"Get up, get up!" Mama ripped my warm covers right off me. "We're going to be late."

Beep, beep, beep.

My alarm sounded just in the knick of time. I was happy to see that Mama was there on time to take me and Finn to the airport. And she was in a very good mood, which made me much happier. Duke was snuggled up next to me. The excitement of leaving to meet Finn's parents was building up in my stomach. I was surprised at the little giggle that escaped my body.

"I have to admit that when the weathermen get it wrong," DJ Nelly chirped through my alarm clock radio, "they get it wrong. But not this winter wonderland."

"Winter wonderland?" My head jerked to the side and I bolted out of bed.

"Stay safe out there and bundle up if you're headed out to the fair grounds." The radio played "Let It Snow".

"No. No. No," I begged and ran across my cold bedroom floor, jerking open my curtains. "No." My heart sank into my gut when the thick blanket of snow made me realize my worst nightmare.

"Honey, don't forget to make your bed. You never know if

the fire department is called and they have to come in while we're gone to the pageant since you can't get to Chicago because the airport is closed."

No wonder she was so chipper. She'd gotten her way. Vivian Lowry had gotten her way, again.

"Come on, Duke," my voice was flat. My phone was on the counter in the kitchen and I wondered what Finn thought.

The murmur down the hall told me she wasn't alone. I grabbed my robe off the chair and threw it on, tying it as I walked down the hall.

"Ah oh, you look mad. When you get mad, you get ugly." Mama had on a full face of makeup and bright red lipstick. "God don't like ugly, Kendrick."

"I'm sorry." Finn stood up from the chair at the table and put his arms out. "Last night you fell asleep and it'd started to snow. I knew it was going to come pouring down overnight. So I went ahead and called the airport to exchange our tickets for after the new year."

"It's all worked out." Mama clasped her hands together.

I melted into Finn's arms and cried not only for me and him, but all the pain and suffering Cottonwood had felt for the loss of Leighann Graves, plus the fact I didn't get to say goodbye to Poppa. I'd been keeping it all inside.

"I'll just be going. Your daddy is waiting for me in the car," Mama whispered. "I'll see you at the pageant."

I felt Finn give a nod and heard the door open, the click of Duke's nails across the kitchen linoleum floor, and the door shut.

"Is she gone?" I asked.

"Yes." Finn took his finger and lifted my chin up so our eyes met. "It's no big deal."

"It is a big deal. I really wanted to meet your family." I took a step back and wiped my face. "I needed to get out of Cottonwood and let this whole Leighann thing get behind me." I gestured between us. "We need to get out of Cottonwood and take a break."

"And we will." He walked over to the coffee pot and poured a couple of cups. "I promise. Besides, I'm looking forwards to watching your mom do that wave thing on stage this morning."

"I'm going to get a kick out of her trying to keep that crown on her head when she's serving the annual Christmas lunch at the undercroft." Both of us laughed. "You get Duke in and feed him while I go get ready."

While getting ready, I'd gotten to the point where I'd accepted the fact the plans had changed back to my old plans. There was some joy knowing that Finn was going to get to experience Christmas with me and my family along with the great town we protected. When Vivian Lowry was involved it was an experience like no other.

Keeping with the spirit, I turned up the radio and listened to DJ Nelly play the Christmas music while I got ready. With my jeans tucked into my snow boots, I headed down the hall. There was a note on the table alongside my coat that said to come outside when I was finished getting ready.

I locked the back door, figuring Duke was with Finn because he wasn't darting around the snow in the backyard and walked through the gate up to the front of my house.

"Merry Christmas." Finn was standing up in a red sleigh that was attached to two horses and a driver. Poppa was sitting next to the driver in his most glorious of ghost forms with Duke sitting next to him.

"Ding, ding," Poppa said and grinned from ear-to-ear,

making fun of me. "What's that saying about when you hear a bell ring an angel gets his wings?"

Ding, ding, ding.

The driver tugged on the string that was attached to a bell on the sleigh.

"Merry Christmas, Kenni-Bug," Poppa waved and disappeared.

"Merry Christmas, Poppa," I whispered looking up into the sky as the big snowflakes tumbled to the ground.

"Ready?" Finn put his hand out. "I wanted you to have that experience you had with your Poppa the first time they had the Christmas Festival at the fairgrounds. I can't drive or even ride a horse, so this'll have to do."

He stuck his hand out and helped me into the sled.

"You did good, Finn Vincent." I wrapped my arms around him and kissed him before the driver said it was time to go.

The wind whipped around us when the driver had the horses go.

"He did do good, Kenni-Bug," the wind whispered in my air. I tugged open the quilts sitting between me and Finn, snuggling up underneath.

The lights that were strung between the carriage lights along Main Street twinkled even more against the white background. The spirit of Christmas began to fill every part of my being with each sound of the horses' hooves hitting the impacted snow.

"Is it how you remember it?" Finn whispered as we made our way onto the fairgrounds.

"Even better." I snuggled closer. "Better than I remembered."

The tent was filled with a standing crowd. The sled had

come to a halt and I took a moment to look around.

There were many fire pits going with people standing around and listening to the carolers sing as they passed. Cottonwood was welcoming Christmas and all it had to offer. No amount of snow could dampen the spirit of this small town.

"May I?" Finn held his hand out. Duke jumped out before me. "We don't want to miss our front row seats."

"What is up your sleeve?" I asked.

"You aren't very good with surprises." He was right. I think that's why I was so good at being a sheriff. I liked to keep the peace, know what was going on and no surprises.

I took his hand and got out of the carriage. We held hands and walked up to the fairgrounds' metal building that was used for the crafts during the summer and the display of pies during the pie competition. He opened the door and Jolee was just inside. Duke jumped and danced around her until she bent down.

"There you are. The show is about to start," Jolee said and gave Duke some good scratches.

I glanced up and the entire inside looked like the basement of Luke Jones's movie theater basement. There was a sheet hung up and just enough chairs for me and my girlfriends.

"Enjoy your annual *White Christmas* movie," Finn whispered in my ear.

"You did all this?" I asked in disbelief.

"He sure did. In a few short hours too." Luke nodded and handed me a big bag of popcorn that was littered with melting chocolate chips on the top. "Jolee has your Diet drink waiting for you too." Jolee waved from the front.

"Thank you." I turned around to look at Finn. There were tears in my eyes. "No one has ever done something so nice for me."

"No one has ever loved you as much as I love you." He bent down. Our lips met in a soft and warm kiss. "Go have fun. I'll be hanging outside."

"You've got you a good one right there." Jolee slipped her arm into mine and we walked up to the seats.

"Yeah." I sighed. "He's a good one."

The entire time "White Christmas" played, and Bing Crosby danced alongside Rosemary Clooney, I watched my friends. Then I wondered what I'd be doing if I was in Chicago with Finn's family. No matter what I'd been doing there, fun or not, I'm sure I'd been thinking about what my friends and family were doing here. I wasn't sure what next year would bring, but I did know that right now, I was truly grateful for the blizzard. This was exactly where I was supposed to be.

Just like Finn said, he was outside waiting for me and Duke.

"Let's go under the tent." He nodded towards the big crowd, hoots and hollers and some whistling. "It looks like we just got here in time."

Duke trotted beside us, sniffing everyone's feet and dangling gloved hands.

Finn pointed to the stage.

"And the winner of this year's is..." Edna Easterly slowly ripped open the red envelope and peeked inside. Mama stood up on the stage in a long red cape with white trim. She and Viola White were holding hands like you'd see on the Miss America pageant.

"Lord help us all if Mama wins," I curled up on my toes and whispered in Finn's ear. He smiled.

"Viola White!" Edna Easterly screamed in the microphone.

Mama had already begun her walk and wave, for sure thinking she'd won the title. Viola practically shoved Mama out of the way and stepped right on up to get that crown from Mayor Ryland and batch of flowers from Myrna Savage.

Mama was a pitiful sight as the disbelief showed on her face. True Southern Mama style, she drew back her shoulders, planted a smile on them bright lips and began to clap. When Viola caught wind of Mama, she started to really prance around the stage and blow kisses.

"Ah oh," Finn said in a scared voice. "Is this going to be a good Christmas?"

"Mama is going to be a sour puss all day," I said as we made our way over towards the edge of the stage where all the contestants were walking off. Duke had already beat us up to the front.

"I swear you paid them off," Mama scoffed.

"I did not." Viola gripped the bouquet of flowers. "They know a real beauty when they see one. Inside and out." She poked herself in the chest.

"Now y'all stop your bickering." I shook my head and realized that no amount of spirit that Christmas brought would bring these two to ever see eye-to-eye.

Just then snowflakes had started to fall from the sky. They were even bigger than before. My insides tickled, and I looked up into the falling flakes.

Ding, ding, the faint sound of a bell jingled from above.

"Merry Christmas, Poppa," I whispered knowing Poppa had gotten his angel wings.

"Merry Christmas to you too." Finn pulled me in for a Christmas kiss that was better than any present or trip he could've ever given me.

TONYA KAPPES

Tonya has written over twenty novels and four novellas, all of which have graced numerous bestseller lists including *USA Today*. Best known for stories charged with emotion and humor, and filled with flawed characters, her novels have garnered reader praise and glowing critical reviews. She lives with her husband, three teenage boys, two very spoiled schnauzers and one ex-stray cat in Kentucky.

The Kenni Lowry Mystery Series
by Tonya Kappes

Henery Press Mystery Books

And finally, before you go...
Here are a few other mysteries
you might enjoy:

I SCREAM, YOU SCREAM

Wendy Lyn Watson

A Mystery A-la-mode (#1)

Tallulah Jones's whole world is melting. Her ice cream parlor, Remember the A-la-mode, is struggling, and she's stooped to catering a party for her sleezeball ex-husband Wayne and his arm candy girlfriend Brittany. Worst of all? Her dreamy high school sweetheart shows up on her front porch, swirling up feelings Tally doesn't have time to deal with.

Things go from ugly to plain old awful when Brittany turns up dead and all eyes turn to Tally as the murderer. With the help of her hell-raising cousin Bree, her precocious niece Alice, and her long-lost-super-confusing love Finn, Tally has to dip into the heart of Dalliance, Texas's most scandalous secrets to catch a murderer...before someone puts Tally and her dreams on ice for good.

Available at booksellers nationwide and online

Visit www.henerypress.com for details

BONES TO PICK

Linda Lovely

A Brie Hooker Mystery (#1)

Living on a farm with four hundred goats and a cantankerous carnivore isn't among vegan chef Brie Hooker's list of lifetime ambitions. But she can't walk away from her Aunt Eva, who needs help operating her dairy.

Once she calls her aunt's goat farm home, grisly discoveries offer ample inducements for Brie to employ her entire vocabulary of cheese-and-meat curses. The troubles begin when the farm's pot-bellied pig unearths the skull of Eva's missing husband. The sheriff, kin to the deceased, sets out to pin the murder on Eva. He doesn't reckon on Brie's resolve to prove her aunt's innocence. Death threats, ruinous pedicures, psychic shenanigans, and biker bar fisticuffs won't stop Brie from unmasking the killer, even when romantic befuddlement throws her a curve.

Available at booksellers nationwide and online

Visit www.henerypress.com for details

BOARD STIFF

Kendel Lynn

An Elliott Lisbon Mystery (#1)

As director of the Ballantyne Foundation on Sea Pine Island, SC, Elliott Lisbon scratches her detective itch by performing discreet inquiries for Foundation donors. Usually nothing more serious than retrieving a pilfered Pomeranian. Until Jane Hatting, Ballantyne board chair, is accused of murder. The Ballantyne's reputation tanks, Jane's headed to a jail cell, and Elliott's sexy ex is the new lieutenant in town.

Armed with moxie and her Mini Coop, Elliott uncovers a trail of blackmail schemes, gambling debts, illicit affairs, and investment scams. But the deeper she digs to clear Jane's name, the guiltier Jane looks. The closer she gets to the truth, the more treacherous her investigation becomes. With victims piling up faster than shells at a clambake, Elliott realizes she's next on the killer's list.

Available at booksellers nationwide and online

Visit www.henerypress.com for details

SECRETS, LIES, & CRAWFISH PIES
Abby L. Vandiver

A Romaine Wilder Mystery (#1)

Romaine Wilder, big-city medical examiner with a small-town past, has been downsized and evicted. She's forced to return to her hometown of Robel in East Texas, leaving behind the man she's dating and the life she's worked hard to build.

Suzanne Babet Derbinay, Romaine's Auntie Zanne and proprietor of the Ball Funeral Home, has long since traded her French Creole upbringing for Big Texas attitude. Hanging on to the magic of her Louisiana roots, she's cooked up a love potion—if she could only get Romaine to drink it. But when the Ball Funeral Home, bursting at the seams with dead bodies, has a squatter stiff, Romaine and Auntie Zanne set off to find out who is responsible for the murder.

Available at booksellers nationwide and online

Visit www.henerypress.com for details

36509469R00131

Printed in Great Britain
by Amazon